11-29-12

SO TANGLED A WEB

It is the year 1881, and Rachel
Biddisham is celebrating her success
in becoming a certified teacher.
Little does she know what a tangle
her appointment at the Old Priory
will bring. One of her pupils is the
wilful Alicia who is engaged to
Laurence Knight. But it is the
arrival of the handsome Orlando
Ormerod, the new art master, that
sets off a chain of events which end
with an elopement and a turnaround
in Rachel's romantic attachments.

GILLIAN KAYE

◆

SO TANGLED A WEB

Complete and Unabridged

LINFORD
Leicester

First published in Great Britain in 2003

First Linford Edition
published 2004

British Library CIP Data

Kaye, Gillian
So tangled a web.—Large print ed.—
Linford romance library
1. Love stories
2. Large type books
I. Title
823.9'14 [F]

ISBN 1–84395–309–9

Published by
F. A. Thorpe (Publishing)
Anstey, Leicestershire

Set by Words & Graphics Ltd.
Anstey, Leicestershire
Printed and bound in Great Britain by
T. J. International Ltd., Padstow, Cornwall

This book is printed on acid-free paper

1

The post office was closed, it being early-closing day in Lymstone, so Rachel went through the garden to the family house, next door. She ran in her excitement, and called her mother's name as she opened the door.

'Mama, where are you? Come quickly! I've got my certificate. And where is Father? He must see it, too.'

Rachel's parents were Mr and Mrs Biddisham and they owned the post office and general store in Lymstone, a large, busy village in farming country, two miles from Yatton and not far from Bristol.

And now, on this warm day in July, 1881, Mrs Biddisham came hurrying from the kitchen when she heard her daughter's excited voice. In the parlour, Rachel held out the certificate, then hugged her mother, almost squashing the precious document.

'My dearest girl,' her mother said as she read out the words which proclaimed Miss Rachel Biddisham to be a certificated teacher. 'I am so proud of you and your father will be, too. He is down the back garden seeing to his vegetables with it being early closing day. And you have worked so hard these two years, you deserve your success.'

Rachel had indeed worked very hard. At the age of twelve, she had stayed on at the village school to be a monitor, then the Lymstone schoolmaster, Mr Grainger, had asked her to help with the infant class, the babies, as they called them. And so Rachel had stayed until she was sixteen, teaching the babies their letters and their numbers. She had loved it and it had not taken much persuasion from Mr Grainger for her to go into nearby Yatton in the evenings and then on Saturday mornings, to travel by the train to Bristol, to do her teacher training.

She had learned geometry, algebra

and decimals as well as the usual English, history and geography. That day, the course had finished and she had travelled back to Lymstone with her precious certificate.

'Run and tell your father,' Mrs Biddisham said.

She was beaming with delight, for although she knew she should not have favourites amongst her children, Rachel was her youngest, her only girl and was very dear to her. Her two eldest boys were nearly ten years older than Rachel and had long since married and made their homes in Bristol.

'I can't believe it's true,' Rachel said. 'I thought the day would never come. I will go and find Father and we must have a celebration. Find a bottle of sherry, Mama. I won't be very long.'

At eighteen years of age, Rachel was a good-looking rather than a pretty girl. She despaired of her long, fair hair which was at times uncontrollable. So she kept it in a thick plait which she fastened to the top of her head with hair pins for special occasions. Her hair when drawn back from her face showed to advantage her fine features and her lively blue eyes, a pale blue, almost grey.

Out in the back garden, she could not stop herself from running. The post office and their house next door had a large piece of land at the back and beyond the orchard, Mr Biddisham happily tended his fruit and vegetables.

'Father,' Rachel called, quite out of breath as she reached him, 'I've done it. I'm a certificated teacher now.'

Mr Biddisham, a tall man in his late fifties, straightened up and beamed at his daughter much as Mrs Biddisham had done. She gave him the piece of paper, and he read the words carefully. Then he stuck his fork in the ground, put an arm round his daughter and kissed her on the cheek.

'Congratulations, my dear, we are proud of you.'

This show of affection from Mr Biddisham was rare for he was a serious and reserved man. He had been the post master in Lymstone for many years and was well respected in the village where he was also church warden.

For the rest of that day, Rachel looked forward to the usual Saturday evening visit from Tom Caldicott. Tom was a young man of twenty-four who owned a linen-cum-draper's shop in Yatton, the small country town near Lymstone. The railway had made Yatton prosperous as it was only a very short journey into Bristol. There were many gentlemen who, although they worked in the banks and offices of the city, preferred to bring up their families in rural Somerset.

So it was that when Tom Caldicott's father had died five years before, Tom had taken over the business and made it into a thriving concern. He lived with his widowed mother over the shop.

Tom had met Rachel in the shop for she was often there to buy the good cotton prints and silks and velvets he sold for their dresses in summer and winter. Although she was only sixteen at the time, she had looked older with her fair plait of hair swept up underneath her hat, and Tom particularly noticed her pleasant composure.

He was not a lot taller than Rachel, but he was of sturdy build. His eyes were blue and his sandy hair was slightly unruly which Rachel thought gave him a boyish look. She liked him, but it took months of, 'Good morning, Miss Biddisham,' before he found the courage to ask her if he could come out to Lymstone and take her for a walk one Saturday evening.

Rachel was flattered and the shy romance continued. Two years later, they still walked on a Saturday evening in the summer, and once a month, Tom would come in his trap to Sunday lunch. Then they would drive to the hill beyond Brockley, or on finer days, as far as Cheddar in the Mendip Hills.

By this time, Tom knew he wanted Rachel as his wife, but Rachel thought of him as a very dear brother. She would have been horrified if someone had accused her of leading him on. He had never expressed any particular affection for her and had certainly not made any suggestion of a future life together. So it was that Rachel imagined that he accepted her as a good friend and companion just as she did, and she had enjoyed their walks and outings together.

The news she had for him that evening was to change their relationship but not their friendship.

Tom came into the house to greet her mother and father as he always did, and immediately he was told the news of the day. He was sincere in his pleasure at Rachel's success and shook them all by the hand.

'You are too clever for me,' he told Rachel with a grin.

Rachel laughed.

'Nonsense,' she said. 'It was more hard work than cleverness. In any case, look what a success you have made of

Caldicott's. It was a very modest, little shop in your father's day and you have improved it tremendously. And you bought the shop next door and started selling hats, too. We used to have to go into Bristol if we needed a hat!'

She looked at her mother.

'Mama, you will agree, I know you will.'

Mrs Biddisham smiled and looked at Tom.

'It is true, Tom, and everyone roundabouts would say the same.'

Tom got to his feet to hide his bashfulness and put a hand out to Rachel.

'Are we going for a walk? And is it going to be the mill, the wood or across the fields?'

There were several good walks around Lymstone, but the three he had mentioned were their favourites. Rachel did not hesitate.

'Across the fields, please. The flowers are lovely at the moment.'

It did not take them long to walk

through the village and take the path across the fields that would eventually lead to the Old Priory. This large, imposing house was well-named for it had been build in the grounds of what had once been a Franciscan priory. There were still the remains of the chapel in one corner of the grounds.

The Old Priory had once been owned by the illustrious de Vere family, but when the heir had been killed in the Crimean War, the house had fallen into disrepair. It was saved only by the efforts of a Mr and Mrs Selworthy from London, who bought it for next to nothing and had used their fortune, their enthusiasm and their energies to convert it into a select school for young ladies. The Priory Academy for Young Ladies was its full title, but local people still referred to it as the Old Priory.

That evening in July, as they crossed the fields, Rachel, still with a glow of happiness at her achievement, thought that Tom was unusually quiet. He was a good-tempered young man and never failed to amuse her with some tale or other of the shop.

'What next, Rachel?' he asked her suddenly.

She looked up at him quickly for his voice had sounded uneasy.

'You mean now that I am a trained teacher?' she asked him.

He nodded.

'Yes. Do you mean to stay in the village school or do you have some great ambition? Are you going to move away?'

It was a direct question and Rachel could not give a quick answer. She looked at him curiously.

'Would you mind if I went away, Tom?'

He stopped then, took her hand in his, and turned her to face him. Rachel knew then that whatever Tom was thinking, it was a serious matter. In nearly two years of walks together, he had never as much as tried to hold her hand and certainly not to kiss her. She had respected him for it. Now, she felt a strong grasp and knew that something was bothering him.

'I had hoped, Rachel, when you were a little older, to ask you to become my wife.'

The words hung between them in the warm, summer air and Rachel looked at him askance. He had never given her any hint of his feelings or his intentions, and she felt herself dumbfounded. How could you possibly keep company with a young man for so long and not know that he entertained such thoughts?

'You are very quiet, Rachel,' he said solemnly.

Rachel faltered.

'But, Tom, I don't understand. We have been good friends, like brother and sister, but I . . . well, I supposed that one day I might fall in love with a young gentleman and then I would be married. But I am only eighteen and I feel that the time has not yet come.'

He now had hold of both of her hands and his words came urgently.

'I have not spoken until now, Rachel,

because you were so young. But we do get on very well and I love you. I would like you to be at my side for the rest of my life. I was afraid that your success would take you away from me, that is why I have spoken this evening. Please, don't turn me down.'

Rachel was feeling distressed. The last thing she wanted was to hurt Tom, but she knew that she could never think of him as a husband. In the years she had known him, she had been working hard at her studies. Thoughts of love had been far from her mind except as a distant happiness with someone who would perhaps stir her feelings into a true romance. Had she been wrong in keeping Tom as a good friend? Had it given him the false signal that one day she would want to become his wife?

'Tom, I don't know what to say. I had not thought of our friendship as a romance. You never as much as hinted, and, Tom, what about Sally?'

'Sally?' he echoed.

'Yes, Sally, your little milliner. She is

devoted to you. Surely you must have seen it. You are with her nearly every day and she is so pretty.'

'But she is so young,' Tom replied with a frown.

Rachel gave a smile.

'She is two years older than me, Tom. It is only because she is so tiny that she seems younger. You have to admit that she is pretty, with her lovely dark curls. I am quite envious. And she understands all about the shop and you know that she makes the most beautiful hats. The one I am wearing this evening is one of hers.'

In her sudden enthusiasm, Rachel turned her head to show off the neat straw hat with its golden ribbons and daisies. Her hair was always unplaited on a Saturday evening and fell almost to her waist.

Tom was grinning.

'Rachel, I think you are just as pretty as Sally. She is a good girl, but she is like a little sister to me. And here we are, the two of us with you thinking of me as a brother and me thinking of Sally as a sister! Shall we wait a little while and see what happens? You will probably go off and be the school-mistress of a village school somewhere and I will work hard in the shop. We will continue to be good friends and one day, when the time is right, I will ask you again.'

'Tom, you are too good. You should have lost your temper with me and taken me in your arms and kissed me until I said yes.'

Tom roared with laughter.

'You have been reading too many novels alongside your mathematics, Rachel. You know quite well that I would never behave like that. But I would like to give you a little kiss to show that we are still good friends.'

Rachel sighed as she lifted her cheek for his soft kiss. She did love Tom in one sense, but there was a feeling lurking somewhere inside of her that she would like to have been held close and kissed passionately by someone whom she loved to distraction.

Tom returned to his shop in Yatton, and the next day the Biddisham family attended service at the village church of St John's. Mr Grainger was also there and was delighted with Rachel's good news. He told her that they would talk about it after school the next day and true to his word, they had their talk late in the afternoon the following day. Mr Grainger, a tall, burly man with a beard, was both open and honest with Rachel. He was a family man of about forty years of age and nowhere near to retirement.

'Rachel, as far as I can see, there are two options open to you. I can apply to keep you here as a certificated teacher, but you would have only the charge of infants. I have several years left in which I must try to impart some elements of English and numbers into the older children. You have been an able assistant for over four years and I would recommend to the school gover-nors that your salary should be commensurate with your experience and now your qualification. If you accepted that, you would be able to continue living at home and it may be that is what you would prefer. What views do you have on the matter? I expect you have been thinking about it all weekend.'

Rachel had listened very carefully to what Mr Grainger had said to her and she appreciated his helpfulness.

'Thank you very much, Mr Grainger. You know that I have been very happy teaching the babies here and in many ways, I would like to continue. I am not saying that my qualification has given me big ideas, but I would like to think that I could become the schoolmistress of a small country school where I would have the opportunity of teaching the older children as well. I will make enquiries and tell you what I am going to do before the autumn term begins.'

She paused thoughtfully.

'I would not mind leaving home, even though I would miss Mama and

Father very much. But, after all, a girl has to be prepared to leave her parents when she marries and sets up a new home elsewhere. I am not getting married, but I know that most village schools have a small house attached to it for the schoolmistress, or the schoolmaster and his family, of course, just as you have here at Lymstone.'

'And what about Mr Thomas Caldicott? I thought I sensed a romance going along there.'

Rachel grinned ruefully. Tom had met Mr Grainger after church on a Sunday and Rachel knew that the schoolmaster approved of him.

'Oh, Mr Grainger, Tom has asked me to marry him, but I have turned him down. I am fond of him and he has been a good friend to me, but having worked so hard to get my certificate, I feel that I would like to go on teaching for a little while before I settle down with a husband and family. Do you think that is unreasonable of me?'

'You are only eighteen, Rachel, and

there is plenty of time to be thinking of marriage. Tom is young, too. I am sure he will be prepared to wait if he loves you.'

Rachel did not like to say that she could not imagine Tom as a husband and that she did not feel romantically inclined towards him. She simply repeated Tom's patient words.

'He said that one day, when the time was right, he would ask me again.'

'Splendid,' Mr Grainger replied. 'I knew him to be a young man of good sense. And, Rachel, if you are school-hunting, I have heard that Miss Cooke at Marton is retiring soon. That might be the opening you are looking for.'

Rachel smiled her gratitude.

'Thank you, Mr Grainger. I will make enquiries.'

A few days later, and while Mr Biddisham was shutting up the post office and the shop, Rachel's mother came hurrying through into the house. Rachel was busy getting the tea things together and laying the table.

'Rachel, Rachel,' her mother said and Rachel could hear suppressed excitement in her voice. 'I'm not one for village gossip, and I hear a lot of it in the shop, but don't spread things around, as you know. I call it mischief-making and often these rumours have no foundation. Why are you laughing? I am quite serious.'

'I am laughing because you have heard something and you cannot wait to tell me. Come along, out with it, Mama.'

Mrs Biddisham did her best to remain serious, but it was hard for her to contain her excitement.

'Rachel, I have been talking to Mrs Hargreaves. You know her for she has been housekeeper at the Old Priory ever since it was made into a school. A very good soul she is. Never misses church on a Sunday.'

'And what did Mrs Hargreaves say to put you in a spin, Mama?'

'Well, it seems the girls have gone home for the summer and just at the

19

last minute, Miss Shears, the geography teacher, who was going to take mathematics next term, suddenly announced that she was going to be married and would not be returning in September. What do you think of that?'

Rachel was silent and thinking hard, for she knew the direction of her mother's thoughts. By calling it the Old Priory, she knew that her mother was referring to the Priory Academy for Young Ladies. She and Tom had walked in that direction only a few nights before. The school was highly thought of. Young ladies from wealthy families received their education there and boarded as well. Mr and Mrs Selworthy, the owners, were regarded with great respect in the neighbour-hood. The girls often took their walks through the village and were allowed to call at the post office.

'What are you thinking, Rachel?' Mrs Biddisham said quietly.

'I am not sure, Mama. We all know what an excellent school the Old Priory is and the girls are very well-behaved. I am sure that they receive a very good education. You are thinking that perhaps I could apply for the post of mathematics teacher, but I am not sure. Would Mr and Mrs Selworthy want someone whose only experience was in the village school? The Old Priory is very select, and I am young. Some of the older girls must be approaching my age.'

'But, Rachel, that might be to your advantage. Mr Selworthy is very forward looking and might welcome a teacher who had something in common with his girls.'

'But, Mama, the girls come from well-to-do families and perhaps would look down on me.'

Mrs Biddisham shook her head.

'No, Rachel that is not so. The girls at the Old Priory are, for the most part, from the families of the wealthy merchants of the city. It is considered the thing for their daughters to be sent to select academies. Girls from the upper classes, the gentry if you like, are educated at home. I believe they are taught music and art and little else. They are taught how to go on in society. You must realise yourself that education is changing for women. You yourself have been able to take classes to be a teacher, which would have been unheard of a few years ago when I was a young girl.'

'Mama, how do you know all this?'

'I listen, my dear, and I read your father's newspaper.'

Rachel chuckled.

'You listen but you don't gossip, Mama. You are a wise mother. You are going to persuade me to apply for the post at the Old Priory, I do believe.'

'And why not?'

'I don't know. I had set my heart on a little village school of my own and Mr Grainger says that there is a vacancy at Marton.'

Rachel was still thinking hard and with an underlying thrill of excitement at the possibility of becoming a teacher at the Old Priory.

The next day, she talked to Mr Grainger about it. He was enthusiastic and promised to give her a good reference. By the evening, the letter to the school was written, putting herself forward as a possible candidate for the teaching vacancy.

2

The letter to the Old Priory written, Rachel had to decide on the best way to send it. She did not relish taking it to the house herself and yet it seemed foolish to post to an address in the same village.

After school the next day, she solved her problem by giving a sixpence to one of the older and more responsible boys and asking him to take it to the Old Priory for her. He set off immediately and very willingly.

Rachel then set herself to wait patiently for a reply if she was going to receive a reply at all. The more she thought about teaching at the academy, the more she liked the idea. Her patience was not to be tested for very long, for when she arrived home from school the following day, it was to find a smiling Mrs Biddisham rushing from the shop to the house, waving a letter.

'Rachel, Mr Selworthy himself, he came into the post office so gentlemanly and asked if he might leave a letter for you. I told him you were at the school and he said to give it to you as soon as you came home. Then he spoke to your father. I overheard some of it. Did we consider that you were an intelligent girl and how was it you had come to study mathematics? Oh, and lots of other things. Very pleasant he was. But read the letter, Rachel, and see what he has to say.'

Rachel was smiling, not only at her mother's excitement, but at that note which she was reading.

'He thanks me for my letter and asks me to attend for interview this coming Saturday afternoon if that would suit me. He ends by saying that he and Mrs Selworthy look forward to meeting me. It sounds quite promising, Mama. What do you think I should wear?'

Mrs Biddisham considered.

'You need to strike just the right

note. Nothing too frivolous and not too plain as to look severe. You need to look well-dressed, Rachel.'

Rachel nodded.

'I think the answer is that dark blue bombazine dress with the pleated skirt and over it I could wear the wool jacket which the tailor made for me last year. It is still quite fashionable and I think I would feel confident in it. Do you think I should wear a hat, Mama?'

'Wear a hat? Of course you must.'

Mrs Biddisham sounded shocked and Rachel grinned.

'Yes, I expect you are right. I will put my hair up and wear that velvet toque which matches the jacket so well.'

Saturday came, and Rachel dressed carefully in the clothes she had planned to wear. She studied herself in her mother's cheval mirror and was satisfied. Her father offered to take her in the trap he used for making deliveries from the shop, but she declined the offer telling him that it was less than a mile to the Old Priory and she could easily walk there. He did not insist, kissed her on the forehead and wished her success.

The gates to the Old Priory were at the far end of Lymstone and all Rachel had to do was to walk down the long, straight drive to the house. She could imagine the carriages and phaetons of years ago travelling in style to visit the de Vere family and thought how times had changed since Queen Victoria had come to the throne. The railway seemed to have taken the place of the family carriage, although the splendid barouches could still be seen travelling between the big country houses.

As Rachel approached the house, she looked at it critically. She had known it all her life, but had never been inside. It had been built in the heyday of the great Georgian period and was indeed very gracious. There was a flight of steps up to the pillared portico of the imposing front door.

I wonder if I should go to the front door or round to the servants' entrance,

Rachel was asking herself when she suddenly became aware of voices raised in argument. She had reached the end of the drive and was aware that on either side of her was a shrubbery with tall, clipped laurels and box hedges. She had no wish to pause or eavesdrop, but the voices from the other side of the laurels were strident. They seemed to come from just two people for she could pick out the high, querulous voice of a young lady and the deeper and somewhat angry voice of a gentleman. When she caught his next words, she imagined him to be a young gentleman.

'Of course we cannot be married from the Old Priory, Alicia. What would your parents think?'

'I don't care what my parents think. They are of the opinion that I am marrying beneath me because I have chosen a banker as my future husband. Because my mother is Lady Elford, she seems to think that I should marry an earl or a baronet at the very least, but I want to marry you, Laurence, and I want to marry you here at the Old Priory.'

Rachel could not take another step forward. She was rooted to the spot by the petulant voice of the young lady who seemed to be the spoiled daughter of Lord and Lady Elford. It was not only that she was intrigued by the conversation, for in truth, she knew she was eavesdropping, but if she moved forward, out of the shelter of the shrubbery towards the front door, she would be seen by the quarrelling pair on the other side of the bushes, and they would know that their quarrel had been overheard.

'Alicia, will you listen to me, please? I have every respect for your father and if your mother is strict, then I admire her for it. I certainly do not want to start our married life with a disagreement about where the wedding is to be held. It has always been a tradition that a young lady is married from her parents' home and in her own church. In your case, it would be from Elford Court and presumably the church at Brompton St Mary.'

There was a pause and Rachel took a step forward, but was quickly halted by an angry and tearful response from the one called Alicia.

'You are not considering my wishes at all, Laurence. Indeed, I am sure I do not know why I wish to marry you, except of course, you are the only gentleman to have asked me. Oh, maybe this is impolite of me, but I am determined not to be married from Elford Court with the mood Mama is in at the moment.'

The gentleman's voice was taut and stiff.

'Would you prefer to cry off, Alicia?'

The female voice rose to a shrill screech.

'No, of course I do not wish to cry off. Being married to you is the only way I have of getting away from home. Oh, lose your temper with me if you like. It would not be the first time.'

'If you wish to speak to me further, Alicia, or would like to apologise, you will find me round at the stables.'

Rachel did not realise that she had been holding her breath, but when she heard the sound of hasty footsteps over gravel, she knew that she must move quickly or she would be seen by the young lady. She hurried up to the front door, but before she had time to raise her hand to the knocker, she heard that same haughty voice behind her.

'The servants' entrance is at the back of the house.'

Rachel wheeled round and tried not to show her shock or her embarrassment. Before her stood a very tall girl, dressed in a fashion which she thought would have been more suited to a garden party. She was wearing a dress of pale pink and with a dozen or more flowers edged with lace around the hem. Under a pretty bonnet trimmed with real flowers was the face of a very beautiful girl whose looks were, at that moment, marred by a haughty frown.

So this is Alicia, Rachel thought. She is probably the Honourable Alicia Dunning if her father is Lord Elford, for Rachel knew that Dunning was the Elford family name. I wonder who the gentleman was, but I must reply. I can be superior, too.

'Thank you very much,' she said coolly and with a tilt of the head. 'I have come to see Mr Selworthy and do not wish to keep him waiting.'

And ignoring the surprised look on the girl's face, she turned and knocked on the door sharply. From the corner of her eye, Rachel saw Alicia hurrying round to the stables, presumably to find her fiancé, whoever he might be.

A maid opened the door and took her across a large entrance hall, rich with Persian rugs and oil paintings. Then she paused at a door and whispered, 'May I ask your name, miss?'

'Miss Rachel Biddisham.'

She was shown into what was obviously the library and greeted by a very tall man, rather gaunt, but not old.

He began to rise from his desk.

'Miss Biddisham, I am pleased to meet you and to welcome you to the Old Priory Academy. Do sit down and I will let Mrs Selworthy know that you are here.'

He turned to the maid.

'Patty, please, will you tell Mrs Selworthy that Miss Biddisham has arrived and that we are in the library?'

Rachel liked him immediately. She liked his quiet manner and the way in which he had spoken to the maid. She felt encouraged. Then she heard him addressing her quietly.

'Miss Biddisham, I will explain the circumstances before my wife comes in, then we can all discuss the situation. The girls, over thirty of them at the academy, have all returned to their homes for the summer break. We had thought to be fully staffed for the next term but Miss Shears, the geography teacher who was to begin a new course in mathematics for the older girls, announced that she was going to be married and would not be returning in the new term. We were not best pleased as it is usual to give at least half a term's notice. However, we were pleased to receive your letter and . . . '

He broke off as the door was opened.

'My dear, here is Miss Biddisham,' he said to the lady who stood there.

She was almost as tall as her husband, but seemed younger. She was thin and erect, but not severe, with an intelligent face. She smiled at Rachel.

'Miss Biddisham,' Mr Selworthy said, 'may I introduce you to my wife, Mrs Adelaide Selworthy? We are co-directors of the academy.'

Mrs Selworthy held out her hand and Rachel shook hands formally. She felt very nervous but was determined not to show it. Mr and Mrs Selworthy sat together at the desk with Rachel in front of them.

'Tell us a little about yourself, Miss Biddisham, and why you think you would be suited to teach mathematics at the academy. You have taught mathematics before?'

Rachel's heart sank. This was not a good start.

'I have taught only the rudiments of numbers to the small children at St John's School here in Lymstone, but for the past two years, I have been going into Bristol for classes at the training college. Mathematics was one of my subjects and now I have my certificate.'

'And tell us what the mathematics consisted of.'

'As well as the basic arithmetic, I studied geometry, algebra and decimals,' she replied quietly.

'And you like the subject?'

'Yes, I do. I have been used to helping my father in the post office and I think numbers have always appealed to me.'

'Good, good. Now I will explain a little about the academy. We call it an academy rather than a school because the girls who come here are young ladies rather than schoolchildren. Their ages range from fourteen to eighteen and we have divided them into two grades. Only the girls in the higher grade will take mathematics. They are, for the most part, daughters of the businessmen of Bristol. They will probably marry into the business world and in these days of education and emancipation of women, they will be expected to have a semblance of learning and polish. One or two of our girls have already gone on to the women's colleges of Oxford and Cambridge, and we have a girl now who hopes to go to Somerville College. If you come to us, she will be one of your pupils.'

He stopped for a moment and looked at his wife.

'Perhaps you would like to explain about the subjects we teach.'

Mrs Selworthy smiled.

'My husband is being modest, Miss Biddisham. He has the running of the academy in his hands and I must tell you that he is a gifted musician. All the music teaching is done by him and the girls are taught about the great composers as well as learning the piano or any other instrument they choose. Now as far as the other subjects are concerned, I am in charge of History and English, and if you come as mathematics teacher, you would also be expected to take geography and science with the younger pupils. You are qualified in these subjects?'

'Yes, I have studied them all,' Rachel replied, beginning to feel more hopeful. 'The only subjects we did not touch at college were music and art.'

'Very satisfactory. Music is taken care of, and we have a new young gentleman coming to us from Bristol for one day a week next term. He is young but he has studied at the Slade School and we are pleased with him. The only subject we have not mentioned is needlework. It is taken care of by our good housekeeper, Mrs Hargreaves, who also teaches a little domestic economy. Now I think we have told you everything. Is there anything you wish to ask? We will discuss salary if we decide that you are suited to the post.'

Rachel was now feeling that she must get this post. She liked the open manner of the Selworthys very much and admired their ideals.

'Would you expect me to live at the school, or would you prefer me to come each day and continue living at home?'

Mrs Selworthy did not hesitate.

'I am afraid that the post depends on you living at the Old Priory and being prepared to join in music, and maybe even drama, in the evenings. If you expect a teaching post which finishes at four o'clock and gives you weekends free, then I am afraid we cannot consider your application. You would have one free evening in the week and alternate Saturdays and Sundays off. This may sound harsh, but the work is not difficult and the salary is generous. What do you say, Miss Biddisham?'

'I am quite prepared to live away from home. My parents know that if I do not succeed in obtaining this post with you, then I shall try for a small country school which offers its own house.'

Rachel wondered if she had said the right thing.

'And do you have any romantic attachments, Miss Biddisham?'

Forgive me, Tom, Rachel thought before she replied.

'I do have a friend who has asked me to marry him, but I have told him that I wish to teach for a few years before I settle down to married life.'

Mr Selworthy stood up.

'Miss Biddisham, I find that is a very satisfactory reply. I will take you into the entrance hall and ask you to sit and wait while Mrs Selworthy and I consider what you have told us.'

In the hall, sitting and staring at the pictures of heavy and rather sombre landscapes, Rachel almost shivered in apprehension.

I would like to come here, she kept thinking. It is a great challenge, but it is a wonderful opportunity, and she offered up a little prayer of hope.

Her thoughts were interrupted by the sound of footsteps coming down the stairs, and she looked towards the broad oak staircase to see a young gentleman hurrying down. He was tall and if not handsome, his looks were striking. He wore his dark hair long and his eyes were a brooding brown, almost black. He looked out of temper, she thought, but when he saw her sitting there, he stopped his hurried steps and his expression changed. Rachel was not to know that in her full pleated skirt, elegant jacket and matching hat, she looked quite charming.

'Hello,' he said as he reached the bottom step, 'or I suppose I should be formal and say good afternoon. Are you the teacher who has come for the mathematics post? Why, you hardly look old enough. Have I offended you? Why are you staring at me as though you have seen a ghost?'

Rachel was staring at the gentleman

because she knew without question from his speech that this was the person she had heard, earlier that afternoon, behind the laurels, losing his temper with the young lady.

Who could he be, she was asking herself. Certainly not one of the teachers the Selworthys had described when telling her how the subjects were allocated.

'I am sorry,' she started to say, and was saved from having to make a reply by Mrs Selworthy coming from the library.

'Miss Biddisham ... oh, hello, Laurence. Miss Biddisham, this is my younger brother, Laurence. Please, come back into the library. We have some good news for you.'

Rachel tore her eyes away from the gentleman standing at the foot of the stairs. She was thinking that he looked too young to be a brother of Mrs Selworthy, but she now knew that indeed he was the Laurence of the overheard quarrel. She followed Mrs

Selworthy into the library and concentrated on what was being said to her.

It was Mr Selworthy who spoke.

'Miss Biddisham, I have to tell you that we are most satisfied with your qualification and with your pleasant personality. I think perhaps we had been looking for someone a little older, but on reflection, Mrs Selworthy and I are both of the opinion that you will have a greater understanding of the problems of some of the older girls. We are thinking of one girl in particular who is aiming for Somerville, but is inclined to be flighty.'

He looked at his wife.

'You will tell Miss Biddisham of the arrangements we would like to make?'

Rachel was feeling a glow of pleasure and achievement and had to listen carefully to what Mrs Selworthy was telling her.

'Our next term starts on September first as we have told you, but the girls will be arriving back a few days before that. We hope that it will suit you to come to us a week before that date in order to learn our methods and arrangements. You will have a small bedroom, with a sitting-room attached. We think that is necessary if you are preparing lessons or marking the work that the girls will be doing. Is that agreeable to you, Miss Biddisham?'

Rachel nodded almost numbly.

'Yes, thank you, Mrs Selworthy. You are most considerate.'

'Not at all. I like to think that we take care of our staff. Now, it is just a question of seeking a reference from Mr Grainger and I am sure he will speak well of you. We will then send you a contract and I hope that the terms will prove acceptable to you.'

Mr and Mrs Selworthy stood up and they all shook hands. Then, before Rachel knew what was happening, she was stammering her thanks and was outside, walking down the drive with her head in the clouds. She could not believe her good fortune. The next moment, she heard hurrying footsteps on the drive behind her and the sound of her name being called.

'Miss Biddisham.'

She turned quickly and to her astonishment saw the figure of the gentleman she knew only as Laurence and who was Mrs Selworthy's brother. He was walking quickly towards her. He stopped at her side and looked at her earnestly. Her blue-grey eyes met his deep gaze and she felt at a loss. She had heard too much in that conversation in the shrubbery.

'Miss Biddisham, please wait. There is something that puzzles me. Why did the sight of me back at the house give you such a shock? I could see it plainly in your face and I am quite intrigued.'

I can never tell him, Rachel thought. I will try to divert the conversation.

'I am afraid that I do not know your name, sir, except that Mrs Selworthy called you Laurence,' she said coolly.

'I am Mr Laurence Knight and as Adelaide told you, I am her brother. We come from a large family. She is the eldest and I am the youngest.'

'You live at the Old Priory, Mr Knight?' she asked tentatively and hoped that she was not sounding too inquisitive.

'No, I have the use of what used to be the gamekeeper's lodge and it suits me very well at the moment.'

Rachel could see the house set back from the main gates, a miniature of the Old Priory, small but elegant. But this had not helped her for she had no idea what to say next unless she talked about her appointment.

'I am hoping to come to the academy to teach mathematics in September,' she said.

It sounded forced and did not succeed in deflecting Mr Laurence Knight from his intention.

'So that is what Adelaide meant when she said that she had good news for you. I congratulate you. My sister and her husband are most particular in whom they appoint to their staff. But I can see that you are trying to evade my question. Have we met before?'

'No, I am sure we have not.'

'You are determined not to tell me,' he said. 'I will have to try and work it out. Are you prepared to answer my questions?'

'No, I do not think I am.'

Rachel was feeling more embarrassed, and now thinking him impertinent.

'I am sure I have never set eyes on you before. I would have remembered your poise and your good looks and lovely eyes.'

His voice was playful and she ignored his tone, disliking him more and more every minute.

'Do you live in Lymstone?'

'I do.'

'You are giving nothing away. Why the secrecy? The sight of me coming down the stairs did not upset you, but as soon as I spoke, you looked alarmed. Now why was that? You had never seen me before yet you knew my voice. The mystery deepens, and as I said, you give nothing away.'

'I will be on my way if you have no objection, Mr Knight.'

Rachel turned away from him, but his hand grasped her arm firmly.

'Something is coming back to me. You must have come for your interview at about the same time as I was walking in the shrubbery with Alicia, my fiancée. I thought I heard steps on the drive, but we started a silly quarrel and I forgot about it.'

His eyes hardened, his grip tightened.

'Did you, by any chance, Miss Biddisham, hear me quarrelling with Alicia? Is that why you recognised me only by my voice?'

3

The voice of Laurence Knight was now both steely and angry, and Rachel tried to shake off his restraining hand.

'I would be glad to be free of your hold, sir. It is hurting my arm.'

He dropped his arm but his expression did not change.

'You have not answered my question. I take it that you were an eavesdropper. I trust that you learned something to your advantage.'

'Mr Knight, you are correct in assuming that I was on the other side of the bushes when you were quarrelling with your fiancée. I had no idea who you were even though I did learn that the young lady was Alicia, the daughter of Lord Elford of Brompton St Mary. The family is known to me. I found myself to be in a very difficult situation. If I went on walking towards the house, you would see me and realise that your conversation had been overheard. If I stayed still, I would have to hope that you would move away and that I would never meet you. As it was, your fiancée saw me standing at the front door of the Old Priory and spoke to me.'

'What did she say to you, for goodness' sake?'

Rachel gave a grin.

'She told me where the servants' entrance was.'

He groaned.

'There are times when I wonder why I fell in love with the girl. She might be beautiful, but she is hardly gracious. So you heard the contents of our quarrel? It interests me to know what you thought of the problem in question. Do you think it proper for Alicia to be married from the Old Priory? Be honest. I am not as fierce as perhaps you have thought me to be.'

Rachel looked at him, easier now that she had made her confession.

'I have never known of a girl being

married from any other place than her parents' home. Miss Dunning seems to have had a disagreement with her parents over her marriage. I somehow feel that Lady Elford must feel it an affront that Alicia wishes to be married from the Old Priory.'

'You are quite correct. As far as Lady Elford is concerned, Alicia is marrying beneath her. The fact that I am a successful banker with a pleasant house in lovely grounds does not seem to weigh with the Elfords.'

'You work in Bristol?'

Rachel did not know why she asked the question.

'Yes. I take my trap to Yatton station where they have suitable stabling, and catch the train to Bristol. I work for a merchant banker and our offices are near enough to be able to walk from Temple Meads station. I could buy a house in Bristol, which is what Alicia wishes, but my sister and I were brought up on a large estate in Hampshire and although I enjoy my work, I find the city stifling. It is pleasant to return to the Old Priory.'

He stopped and stared at her.

'Why on earth am I telling you all this? I should be feeling appalled because our quarrel was overheard, yet I am telling you the story of my life.'

Rachel felt confused. Her feelings for this young man were alternating too quickly. First there was the guilt, then the admiration, followed by dislike, and now a quickened interest. But she was truthful.

'I think perhaps it is because I have been accidentally catapulted into your private life. I apologise for that and I can assure that what I have learned will go no further. I bid you good afternoon, Mr Knight.'

Again his hand went to her arm, but this time the gesture was gentle although she could feel the pressure of his fingers through the cloth of her fine wool jacket.

'May I walk a little way with you, Miss Biddisham? And I would like to know your name. We seem to have jumped the bounds of formality with each other.'

His voice was polite and proper, but Rachel felt that he was too familiar.

'The answer to both is no, Mr Knight. Should Miss Dunning see us walking down the drive together, she would be incensed and rightly so,' she replied swiftly and set off to walk to the gates, but she found him still at her side, though he had released his hold on her arm.

'I will come as far as the gates for I find myself wanting to know more about you and I also have to give you a warning. I am returning to the lodge in any case, and if Alicia sees me, she will know that I am on my way home.'

'But I don't understand. Surely Miss Dunning will be wanting to speak to you after your quarrel and I suppose she will be wanting to go home to Elford Court.'

'You are wrong in both of your assumptions,' he said lightly. 'Alicia will be in a sulk for the rest of the evening, and she is staying at the Old Priory.'

'Do you mean that she has really disagreed with her parents?'

Rachel found herself wanting to know more.

'It is not just that, and it is one of the reasons I wanted to speak to you, to warn you, as I said. Alicia will be one of your pupils.'

In her astonishment, Rachel stopped and turned to look at him.

'What can you mean?' she asked him. 'She must be older than I am.'

'I do not know your age, ma'am, but Alicia is just eighteen. She was educated at home, but her parents sent her to the academy for music and art and a little extra polish. They also thought that she should learn mathematics and science.'

'But she will never agree to be my pupil. She thought I was a servant.'

'Alicia will have to agree, and she can be very charming when she chooses to be. I will tell you that we fell in love when we first met just a year ago, but we waited until her eighteenth birthday before becoming engaged. Now, as you overheard, we are planning our marriage. Ah, I can see that you are thinking she will never make me a good wife, but I can assure you that as well as being beautiful, she can be good fun when she chooses.'

'I hardly think that she will be good fun in a mathematics lesson,' Rachel said drily.

He smiled at her.

'One of the reasons that I wished to walk the length of the drive with you was because I had the feeling that you would be a good influence on Alicia. I also feel I would like to know you a little better. It is not every day that one meets a mathematics teacher as lovely as you are.'

Rachel laughed aloud.

'I know, sir, from my own mirror, that I can never be described as beautiful. You choose to flatter me because you wish me to use my influence on your Alicia.'

They were still facing one another and, sharing their laughter, their eyes met. An unexpected feeling passed between them and Laurence Knight put up a hand and touched her lightly on the cheek with the tips of his fingers.

'I would like to know your name,' he said quietly.

Rachel was transfixed, gripped by an emotion she could not recognise.

'It is Rachel,' she replied in a whisper.

'Thank you, Rachel,' he said cheerfully, breaking the spell as though deliberately. 'I am pleased to have met you. I think I am almost pleased that you were our eavesdropper. It was meant to be, for a reason we do not know at the moment, indeed may never know. Here we are at the lodge. I will bid you good afternoon and leave Alicia in your safe hands. Farewell.'

Rachel walked home with her head in a whirl. She did not know which was uppermost in her mind, the promise of her post at the Old Priory or her meeting with Mr Laurence Knight.

Her parents were very pleased with her news, and after tea, she went up to her bedroom to await Tom's arrival, as it was Saturday evening and fine enough for their walk. Somewhat to Rachel's horror, however, it was not Tom's face she was seeing in her mind's eye, but that of Laurence Knight.

Something happened, she was thinking. I was prepared to dislike him, but suddenly I could feel the force of his personality and it still seems to be with me now. Instant dismissal, she told herself sternly. You might never meet him again and in any case, he belongs to Miss Alicia Dunning, though it does seem as though the Elfords are not enamoured with the match.

Then she made herself think of Tom. I have a lot to tell him, though I will be careful not to mention the quarrel and the eavesdropping.

It was a fine evening, and Tom said that he would drive her up the hill towards Brockley and they could sit and chat and admire the view.

'You have done well, Rachel,' Tom said when she told him the story of her appointment at the academy.

She smiled at him.

'It just awaits the reference from Mr Grainger, but he has promised to give me a good one. Do you know Mr and Mrs Selworthy, Tom? And did you know that Mrs Selworthy has a younger brother who lives at the lodge at the Old Priory? I discovered that he is going to marry Lord Elford's daughter, who is going to be one of my pupils.'

'I knew that there was a young city gentleman living at the lodge,' he replied, 'but I had no idea that he was Mrs Selworthy's brother. She and Mrs Hargreaves are often in the shop buying materials and bits and bobs for the girls' needlework classes. And I have some news for you, Rachel, also connected to the Old Priory. Mrs Selworthy has been very impressed with our millinery and I told her that Sally made all the hats. The outcome is that Sally is going to teach the girls how to trim their hats. She is going to the Old Priory every early-closing day in the afternoon. I will take her there as soon as I close the shop and go back and fetch her at tea-time. Sally is very pleased with the idea. What do you think?'

Rachel smiled. She, too, was very pleased with the idea of Tom and Sally being involved in the venture. It gave her the hope that perhaps Tom would transfer his affections from her to Sally. She did not say this, but she showed her enthusiasm.

'I think it is a splendid idea and the girls will love making hats. Sally is very clever.'

'You sound very keen,' he observed. 'You are not trying to matchmake, are you, Rachel? You know very well that it is you I wish to marry. I promised not to mention it again for a little while, but it is always in my mind.'

Rachel looked up at Tom and could

see a sincere kindness in his expression. Then, to her alarm, the vision of dark brown eyes came to her and she saw a different face.

'You are very kind, Tom, but don't count on me. You would have more success with your clever and pretty Sally.'

'We shall see,' he said with a grin.

Oh, dear, Rachel thought, he is so good-natured. Why is it that I cannot love him as I imagined I would love the man who would one day be my husband? And it is no use being stirred by the looks of Mr Laurence Knight if he is soon to marry Alicia.

The following few weeks were taken up in a frenzy of dressmaking on the part of Mrs Biddisham and Rachel until it was felt by both of them that she was dressed suitably to be a school mistress at the Priory Academy for Young Ladies.

Although Rachel was leaving home, she felt no heartache at leaving her parents. She knew she would be visiting them on her free Saturdays and Sundays. She felt very excited as her trunk was strapped to her father's trap. She had paid several visits to the Old Priory since her interview and the confirmation of her appointment, and she had been shown over the lovely old house by Mrs Hargreaves. Then Mr and Mrs Selworthy explained the time-table of lessons and she had been shown the small bedroom and living-room which would be hers. On none of these occasions had she seen Mrs Selworthy's brother again and she felt thankful.

Rachel soon settled in and the girls returned to their school over the next few days. She found it an easy way of making their acquaintance. On the day before the term proper and the lessons were due to start, there was still no sign of Alicia Dunning. Mrs Selworthy remarked on it to Rachel.

'I am beginning to wonder if Alicia is going to return. I expect you have heard of her from the other girls. She is a very

60

lively, young lady. She was going to spend the summer break here, but then I think that she and Laurence had a quarrel so she returned to Elford Court. Have you been told that she is to marry my brother, Laurence?'

'Yes, I do know. I met your brother on the day of my interview. Miss Dunning seems rather young for him.'

Mrs Selworthy was inclined to agree.

'She is now eighteen and would be entering into Society if she was still at Elford Court, but she and Laurence insisted on becoming engaged on her eighteenth birthday. We cannot like the match, but perhaps she will not be quite so giddy once she is married. Things are by no means settled. Her parents do not approve of her marrying a banker and Alicia is now refusing to live at the lodge where Laurence has made his home.'

She stopped and hesitated over her next words.

'I don't know that I should be telling you all this, but I must be honest, my dear Miss Biddisham, and tell you that we hope that you will be a calming influence on Alicia. I think she might take more notice of advice from someone of her own age. I really do expect her some time today, and I had better prepare you for our biggest problem. Alicia keeps insisting that she wants to be married from here and not from Elford Court, and that is not at all the thing.'

Rachel had to force herself to be shocked.

'But a girl is always married from her parents' home, Mrs Selworthy.'

'Quite so. I had expected that response from you. See what you can do for us,' Mrs Selworthy replied and got up to leave the room.

After dinner, there was still no sign of Alicia Dunning and Rachel went up to her sitting-room to prepare her time-tables and lessons of the first day of term. She had now met all the girls and found them to be pleasant young ladies with the usual mixture of quiet and shy girls, the show-offs and the seriously intelligent. She noticed with some amusement and interest that this last group was also the nicest-looking of the bunch.

As she put her time-table together, she felt nervous for the first time. Had she really learned enough geometry and algebra to be able to teach it to the older girls? Arithmetic was no problem to her quick brain.

She heard a sharp tap on the door and called, 'Come in', thinking it to be one of the maids or even Mrs Selworthy, but standing there, and looking quite beautiful, was the girl she knew to be Alicia Dunning.

'Hello. Mrs Selworthy sent me up to tell you that I have arrived. Rather late, I know, but there was a hold-up at home. I am the Honourable Miss Alicia Dunning and my father is William Theodore Dunning, fourth Viscount Elford and we live at Elford Court.'

The girl paused and Rachel held her breath. She is certainly beautiful, she was thinking, but I don't think that I am going to like her. She was given no time to say anything.

'I seem to think that I have met you somewhere before, but I cannot think where if you are a teacher. I am to learn mathematics with you, I am told.'

Rachel was feeling on edge, and determined not to feel her irritation at the supercilious voice of Alicia Dunning, she pulled forward a chair.

'Do sit down, Alicia. I have been instructed to call all the young ladies by their first names. Yes, I am Miss Biddisham, and I have come to the academy to teach mathematics and geography. I believe that your parents wish you to learn mathematics.'

Alicia tossed her head. Her hair was as fair as Rachel's but hung in beautiful ringlets to her shoulders. She was wearing a dress of blue printed silk. The skirt was straight to the front, but full and flowing on a bustle at the back, and there was a frill of white lace around the neck.

I don't wonder that Mr Knight fell in love with her, was Rachel's unbidden thought which she immediately dismissed from her mind as she listened to the proud young lady.

'Yes, it is quite ridiculous. I am to be married very soon to Mr Laurence Knight, a younger brother of Mrs Selworthy. My mother, Lady Elford, disapproves, but my father is more lenient. He has always permitted me to do anything I wished. He is of the opinion that if I am to marry a banker, then I should know more than how to run a house and give instructions to the cook. So, Miss Biddisham, you will have me as a pupil for a term or two and I promise to put my mind to what you have to say. Laurence will be pleased. We are not getting along very well at the moment, but he is so handsome and clever. I do not want to have to cry off.'

She smiled and got up.

'I must go and see if Becky has unpacked my trunk. I bring my own maid with me. It makes things much easier as I am most particular about my dresses and hats. Oh, and did you know, Miss Biddisham, that we are to have a milliner here once a week, to show us how to trim our hats? That will be fun for I love hats and the fashion is extraordinary at the moment. Now I must stop my chatter. I think I am going to like you for we must be of an age and you do not look strict. I will try hard with my mathematics.'

She had reached the door and Rachel thought she had ceased her flow of trivial talk. She regarded the girl certainly as a charmer, but she also seemed spoiled and self-opinionated. Rachel opened the door for her visitor and was treated to a pleased remark of satisfaction from her visitor.

'I have remembered where I have seen you before. It was that afternoon that Laurence and I had a quarrel and you were standing at the front door and I thought you were a girl from the village who had come for a post of servant. I do apologise. I had no idea that you were going to be my future mathematics teacher.'

She paused and was, for a moment, lost in thought. Then came the awkward words.

'But, Miss Biddisham, if I met you at the front door, it was immediately after I had quarrelled with Laurence in the shrubbery. You must have been walking up the drive at the time for there was no vehicle. Does it mean . . . did you hear our quarrel accidentally?'

Rachel knew she would have to be honest and hoped she could pass the incident off lightly. There was no need to tell Alicia that she had afterwards met the girl's fiancé and walked down the drive with him.

'Yes, Alicia,' she said quietly. 'As I walked along, I could hear you quarrelling, though of course I had no idea who it was, except that it sounded like a young lady and a gentleman having a lovers' tiff.'

Alicia frowned.

'I wish I could think of it as a tiff. It was over such a silly thing. I would like to be married from here and not from Elford Court, but everyone disagrees and says I must be married from my home. What do you think, Miss Biddisham?'

My problem with Alicia has arisen even before the term has started, Rachel thought. I must do my best.

'Alicia, it is a very old tradition that a girl is married from her parents' home. It would seem most odd if you were to marry from your fiancé's home, and most embarrassing for Lord and Lady Elford. They would be expected to give the wedding breakfast after the ceremony and to entertain the guests.'

She paused and was surprised that she seemed to have Alicia's full attention.

'If Mr Knight is a banker, he must be well respected in the city. I am sure your father would come to appreciate his qualities.'

'My father is not as critical as Mama.

She thinks I should marry a baronet at the very least. Title is everything to her and yet she was only the daughter of a country parson herself. Whatever shall I do? I will agree that it would seem improper to be married from here, yet how can I get Mama to accept Laurence into the family?'

Rachel tried again.

'Alicia, it is not something that has to be decided straightaway. Let Mr Knight impress his attributes on your mother. Let her know how much he cares for you and that he agrees with her that you should be married from Elford Court. She will gradually come to see that he is an estimable young man from a very respectable family and that having a title is not the most important thing in a marriage.'

Alicia looked at Rachel earnestly.

'You seem very wise, and you speak almost as though you know Laurence. Have you met him?'

Be careful, Rachel, she told herself.

'I was introduced to him briefly on

the day of my interview, but have not had the privilege of meeting him since.'

She knew that was being economical with the truth.

'I think he would like you better than he likes me. You are calm and sensible. He thinks I am rattle-brained. But he does love me and he approves of me staying on at the Old Priory to learn mathematics. I shall continue to do English with Mrs Selworthy, and music and art, of course. I am quite good at drawing and painting. Did you know that we are to have a new art master this term? I hope he is young and handsome. Mr Thornton, whom we had last year, must have been about sixty, but he was a very good teacher. I learned a lot from him. Oh, well, Miss Biddisham, I thank you for listening to me. I think I am going to like you for you have been very patient with me. I wish Laurence was as patient as you are. Good-night. I will go and see if Becky has finished unpacking my trunk.'

She was gone and Rachel sat back in her chair and didn't know whether to laugh or cry. That Miss Alicia Dunning was beautiful there was no denying, but it was obvious that she was both wilful and selfish. I will do my best, was all that Rachel could think.

The term started next morning and the first week at the Old Priory went well for Rachel. She took the older girls and found them attentive and eager to learn. Mathematics seemed to be a challenge to them after many lessons of English, art, needlework and music.

Alicia was a surprise to Rachel. The capricious girl had a keen mind when she chose to concentrate, and in just a few days, she became fascinated with the geometry and algebra which Rachel had started to teach her.

On the last day of that first week, they were expecting their new art master from Bristol. All the girls were gathered in the art room, with the exception of Alicia. She and Rachel had been tackling a difficult equation in algebra the day before and surprisingly, Alicia had asked if they could look at it again before the art class began. So it was that Rachel and Alicia were seated at a desk in the usual classroom, when the door was opened and a cheerful Mrs Selworthy stood there.

'Ah, there you are, Alicia. You were missing from the art room, I noticed. This is Mr Ormerod, our new art master.'

And there walked into the room behind Mrs Selworthy, without question, the most handsome young gentleman Rachel had seen in her life. Dressed all in black, and with an extravagant white cravat, his dark hair almost reaching his shoulders, with startling grey eyes in a serious face of classical features, Mr Ormerod stood staring at Alicia.

Rachel glanced in the young lady's direction and saw an expression of shining adoration.

Oh, my goodness, Rachel thought, what next?

4

Rachel looked on at what happened next in the classroom and was fearful of the outcome. Mrs Selworthy, still smiling, drew Alicia forward to meet Mr Ormerod.

'This is one of our most gifted artists, Mr Ormerod. Mr Ormerod, the Honourable Miss Alicia Dunning. She is the daughter of Lord Elford.'

Alicia put her hand into Mr Ormerod's and smiled at him.

'I am pleased that you are going to be our new art master, sir,' she said.

Mr Ormerod, looking as though he had never seen such a beautiful girl, turned to Mrs Selworthy.

'I will take Alicia along to the art class myself.'

The two of them walked out of the room together and Mrs Selworthy looked at Rachel.

'Miss Biddisham, I am sorry that I did not introduce you, but you will meet Mr Ormerod properly when we have our staff meeting. It is our custom to meet every Friday afternoon to discuss the week's progress, and we always make sure it is before the art master has left.'

She paused, lost in thought for a moment.

'Rachel, I believe that we have just been witness to what might be the cause of some bother. Did you see their faces?'

Rachel nodded.

'It was impossible not to see it, Mrs Selworthy. We will have to admit that Mr Ormerod is a very handsome young gentleman. And for all her faults, Alicia is beautiful and can be very nicely behaved.'

'I think the best plan would be to ask Mr Ormerod to make a fuss of all the girls and not just Alicia,' Mrs Selworthy said thoughtfully. 'We are certain to have twenty love-sick girls, and not just

Miss Alicia Dunning. Mr Selworthy and I did not consider the young man's good looks when we appointed him. We were so pleased with his work and qualifications.'

'I am sure he will do very well, and we must not forget, after all, that Alicia plans to marry your brother.'

Mrs Selworthy nodded.

'Yes, I know and I am not sure if I am pleased about the match or not. I am of the opinion that Alicia is too young for Laurence. My brother is a serious young man, but the next few months will show if they are genuinely attracted to one another. The marriage is not planned until the spring.'

When Rachel met Mr Ormerod later that day at the so-called staff meeting, she found him to be sincere and pleasant. She was by no means dazzled by his good looks, and indeed, he seemed unaffected by what many would have called his manly beauty. He reported well of the girls' work and was of the opinion that they had been well and carefully taught.

'Miss Dunning seems to be especially talented,' he told the Selworthys. 'With your permission, I will try and give the last part of my day here to give her individual tuition. It is difficult to help someone so gifted in a class of nearly twenty girls.'

Mrs Selworthy looked at Rachel. The serious suggestion had come from the art master with a genuine enthusiasm. Rachel could understand his meaning, for his day was divided into two classes — the younger girls in the morning and the seventeen and eighteen-year-olds in the afternoon. He had not suggested that he should give Alicia individual tuition and Rachel was of the opinion that if Alicia did have a talent, then she would benefit from extra coaching. She gave a slight nod to Mrs Selworthy who seemed to be waiting for her opinion.

The older lady spoke with her husband and then turned to the art master.

'Thank you, Mr Ormerod. We do not

encourage individual coaching but I do think that Lord Elford would be pleased to see his daughter's obvious talent developed.'

The meeting broke up and Rachel found herself alone with Mr Ormerod who was preparing to return to Bristol. The Selworthys, in their kind manner, had sent one of the stable boys in the trap to see the art master from the train in the morning and taken back to Yatton station at the end of the day.

'I hope you have enjoyed your first day here, Mr Ormerod,' Rachel said, thinking that he looked slightly distracted.

'Yes, yes, I have,' he replied. 'The girls have been well taught, but I was astonished at the talent of Alicia Dunning. She is a very beautiful girl and not empty-headed, it seems. She told me that she was taking mathematics with you, Miss Biddisham,' to which Rachel nodded.

'She is a very bright young lady, slightly spoiled, I think, but her parents wish her to stay on at the academy until the time of her marriage. She is to marry Mrs Selworthy's brother, Mr Laurence Knight, in the spring.'

Mr Ormerod looked startled.

'Married? But she is only a child.'

'They became engaged on her eighteenth birthday.'

'I see. Well, I certainly wish her happiness. And now I must go. I will see you again next Friday, I trust, Miss Biddisham.'

'I will walk to the front door with you, Mr Ormerod,' Rachel replied.

She saw him off and went thoughtfully back into the house to be met by a whirlwind of an Alicia Dunning.

'Miss Biddisham, oh, has he gone? What did you think? Is he not the most handsome gentleman you have ever seen? And so kind and gentle and he liked my painting, too. And did you know that his name is Orlando? Is that not poetic? Orlando Ormerod.'

Alicia gave a sigh, and at once, Rachel felt alarm bells ringing.

'I trust you did not ask him his name, Alicia.'

'Oh, no. I do know how to behave, Miss Biddisham. I saw his name written in a book on sketching which he was showing to me. He was telling me of the importance of making sketches before starting the final picture. He is so clever and kind and charming and, oh, just beautiful.'

'Alicia, you are behaving foolishly. I hope you will not let Mr Knight know of the effect Mr Ormerod has had on you.'

'As if I would. I am not silly, but young ladies always fall in love with their art master.'

'You have been reading too many novelettes, Alicia. Please try and behave in a more seemly manner next Friday.'

'Oh, I will, Miss Biddisham, for I must not upset Laurence again.'

But before the next Friday arrived, it became obvious to Rachel that Alicia had upset her fiancé.

Rachel had spent the Saturday at

home, with lots to tell her parents of her first week at the academy and then met Tom during the evening. Tom was in his usual pleasant mood and seemed particularly pleased that Sally had enjoyed her first efforts at teaching millinery to the young ladies.

On the Sunday of the same weekend, although it was not her free day, Rachel soon found that her duties were not onerous. Attending morning service at St John's with the girls and taking a walk with the younger ones in the afternoon was all she was called upon to do. She was free again in the evening while the girls busied themselves with their needlework, and some of them played the piano or the others to sing.

Alicia, Rachel noted, sat quietly in a corner of the room with her sketchpad and pencil. When she glanced over the girl's shoulder, she could see that Alicia was sketching likenesses of the girls and that the sketches were light and accurate. Seeing that they were all safely occupied, Rachel decided to stroll in the gardens. She felt that she wanted to make the most of the fine weather before the dark evenings set in.

She was in the same shrubbery which had been the scene of Mr Knight's quarrel with Alicia, when she was startled by the sight of Mr Knight himself walking through the shrubs towards her. He stopped with a smile.

'Miss Biddisham, this is fortunate indeed. But I can't go on calling you Miss Biddisham. May I call you Rachel? I discovered that was your name on the last occasion of us meeting, and please, call me Laurence.'

She liked his friendliness, but discovered a reserve in her own manner.

'I think I would prefer to be formal, Mr Knight.'

'Very well, I will wait. But now I must tell you why I am so very pleased to meet you here. I was going to seek you out later on. I am on my way to visit Alicia. Will you be honest with me?'

She was startled by his question and looked up at him in surprise.

'Why, yes, of course I will be if I can. It is not a habit of mine to be dishonest.'

'No, exactly. Tell me, who is Orlando?'

Rachel was taken aback. Surely Alicia had not had the stupidity to talk about the new master, and using his first name, to her fiancé.

'You hesitate, Rachel. Before I say anything else, tell me truthfully what you know about this Orlando.'

'Mr Knight, I feel alarmed. I do know who Orlando is, but you are implying that Alicia has been talking about him.'

'Yes, that is so. I usually see her on Saturdays and Sundays, but not in the week during term time. This weekend, his name has been mentioned in every other sentence.'

Rachel gave an audible groan.

'It is worse than I thought.'

'Tell me, if you please,' he said rather shortly.

'Orlando is Mr Orlando Ormerod,

the new art master and came for the first time on Friday. He is, without question, the most handsome young gentleman I have ever seen.'

'I see. You are not smitten with him, are you?'

'Goodness gracious, no, he is not the kind of gentleman I admire at all,' she said, laughing.

'Thank goodness for that.'

'What do you mean?'

'Never mind for the moment. Tell me more about the handsome art master.'

'He is very good-looking, but he is also very talented and very proper. I have talked to him and found him quite sincere and sensible. Alicia . . . '

She stopped, but he encouraged her to go on.

'Alicia took one look at him and if you had seen her, you would have said that she had fallen instantly in love with him, the foolish girl. Then, I am afraid, without knowing anything about her, he decided that her work was very good and that he would help her. It only needed a little extra attention from him, and praise, of course, quite genuine, to send her into raptures. Then she discovered that his name was Orlando. No, he did not tell her. She saw it written in one of his books, and that seemed to settle things. Orlando Ormerod, artist, was the most romantic person she had ever met. But I am surprised that she has referred to him in front of you, for I particularly warned her not to speak of him to you. Oh, dear, what a silly child.'

'You are referring to the young lady who is to become my wife, ma'am.'

'That is true, but I am afraid to say that Alicia is really taken with Mr Ormerod and she has only met him the one time.'

Rachel felt as though she was not saying the right things.

'I am sorry, Mr Knight.'

'Could you not try Laurence? Mister sounds so formal.'

'Laurence it is then. I am very perturbed about Alicia, but I will say in all truthfulness that I think she will soon forget him. You must realise that he comes only once a week and they are never on their own together. And it is you she loves, after all.'

'I am not so sure about that, and now that I have met you, I am not so sure about myself either.'

Rachel raised her head in alarm, wondering what he meant by his words.

'Whatever are you saying, Mr Knight? I do not understand your words.'

'No, Rachel, I am not free to tell you, but I . . . '

Rachel was never to know what he had been going to say to her, for at that moment, in a whirl of fine cream muslin, Alicia came running up towards them, a large sheet of paper in her hand.

'Laurence, I have been waiting for you. Whatever are you doing here with Miss Biddisham? I hope it is not a flirtation.'

She hardly paused, but gave him the

piece of paper. Rachel saw immediately that it was the sketches of the girls she had seen Alicia working on earlier.

'But look, I have been doing just what Orland . . . oh, I mean Mr Ormerod told me. And they are really good likenesses though I should not say it myself. All my friends are very pleased with them and they want me to do an individual portrait which they can send home. I will become an artist.'

Laurence looked at Rachel before he replied to Alicia, and their eyes met with a degree of understanding passing between them, but he spoke kindly to Alicia, while chiding her at the same time.

'They are excellent, Alicia. I do not doubt that your friends are very pleased. I am pleased, too. It will be a good pastime for you once we are married, but I think I have heard enough of the wonderful Mr Ormerod, and I trust that you are not going to be so foolish as to fall in love with him. If your mother does not approve of a banker, then I cannot begin to think what she would say if you deserted me for the art master.'

Rachel could have laughed aloud at the expression on Alicia's face, but the girl did make a respectful reply to Laurence.

'Well, I suppose I could have fallen in love with him quite easily, but I know that it is not proper and I do love and honour you, Laurence.'

Laurence took Alicia's arm, but spoke to Rachel.

'I am pleased to have met you, Miss Biddisham, and I will now take your pupil off for an evening walk. Shall we walk over to the old ruins, Alicia? We can sit on the stones and talk to each other.'

Rachel watched them go. She had not had the opportunity of exploring the ruined chapel of the priory which lay to the side of the big house and as far as she could see, there was only one wall and part of another remaining upright. But there were lots of other low walls and single stones making up the outline of the original priory. It looked inviting.

She was also interested to see Laurence and Alicia walking together. She was beginning to wonder if he had doubts about his impending marriage. Alicia might be very decorative, and talented with her pencil and paint brush, Rachel was thinking, yet there were times when she seemed to be no more than a foolish child. She had not even had the sense not to prattle on about Orlando Ormerod to Laurence.

Rachel knew herself attracted to Laurence Knight. She could feel a thread of sympathy and understanding between them even though she had met him on only the two occasions. She had never felt like this about Tom and was still in hopes of his attachment to Sally.

With Laurence and Alicia married, and Tom and Sally together, she would be left on her own, but this did not worry her for the moment. Even after only a week at the academy, she knew that she loved her work and was very fortunate.

For two or three weeks, she saw nothing of Laurence Knight and she thought that Alicia had recovered from her infatuation with the art master. The girl was doing some good work both in her mathematics and in her painting. Alicia proved to be not so flighty as Rachel had first thought.

Then in just a few hours, three weeks later, what had seemed to be a settled state of affairs suddenly flared into a situation of emotion and awkwardness for them all.

It was a Friday afternoon and the teaching staff, Mr and Mrs Selworthy and Rachel were gathered in the library for their usual staff meeting. Mrs Hargreaves was always included. Only Mr Ormerod was missing.

'I wonder if he has forgotten,' Mrs Selworthy commented. 'I hope he has not already left for the station. We value his contribution to the meeting.'

'Shall I go and see if he is still in the art room?'

'Yes, please, my dear. We will wait for you.'

If Rachel had known of Miss Alicia Dunning's behaviour during the previous half hour, she thought afterwards that she would not have gone to the art room so readily . . .

That afternoon, as the girls had left the art room, Alicia had stayed on, quietly working, waiting for them all to go. Her heart was in a turmoil over Orlando Ormerod, yet she had never once been on her own with him, and she was wily and bold enough to try and manipulate a few moments by herself in the company of the adored art master.

Orlando was tidying the room before going to the staff meeting. He had given his accustomed half-hour of undivided attention to Alicia and he thought she had gone with the other girls. He was finding it difficult to curb his admiration for her and knew it would not do to seek her out. In spite of his flamboyant looks and dress, he was a quiet and steady young man, and was enjoying the task of teaching the young ladies of the academy.

He took one last glance around the room before leaving and stopped still, startled by the sight of Alicia still seated by the window, painting quietly. It appeared as though she was trying to capture the scene towards the priory ruins which could be seen from the art room.

'Alicia,' he said sharply.

He knew he was speaking sharply because he could feel the thud of his heart as he took in her quiet beauty and poise. It was a feeling that was not permitted to him. He also knew very well that he should not be found on his own with one of his pupils.

Quietly, she put down her brush and looked towards him.

'Oh, Orlando,' she said with a hint of breathlessness.

He walked towards her.

'What are you doing here? I thought you had left with the other girls.'

'I wanted to be on my own with you, just for a few minutes.'

He sat down heavily on a chair near her easel.

'Alicia, you will get up and leave immediately. If I am found with you, I will lose my post.'

'No-one will see us. Come and look at the painting I have been doing of the ruins. It is all faint and mystical. That is what you have been trying to teach me, isn't it?'

'I know very well that it is what I have been trying to say and you are quick to learn, but I will not have you here. Please, go at once.'

'Don't be angry with me,' she simpered. 'You do like me, don't you?'

'Of course I do. You are a lovely girl and you are producing some very good work. Now go.'

She put her brush down and rose, taking a step nearer to him.

'I think I have fallen in love with you.'

She said the words very quietly, raising blue eyes to his. Orlando, knowing that more than anything he wanted to take her in his arms and hold her close, lost his temper. It was something he rarely did, but this young girl had found her way into his heart.

'You have not fallen in love with me, Alicia. You think you have fallen in love with the handsome art master and that is all there is to it. You love Laurence Knight and you are to be married in the spring.'

To his horror, tears trickled down her cheeks.

'I don't love Laurence in that way. He is kind but that is all. Everything has changed since I met you.'

He took his handkerchief from his pocket and put out a hand to wipe away her tears. She raised her own hand to touch his, and on to this scene walked Rachel, coming in search of Orlando. She stood in the doorway and stared in disbelief. Had she interrupted a love scene?

'Alicia,' she found herself shouting. 'Orlando.'

He turned to her with anger in his eyes.

'Rachel, will you tell this silly girl to leave the room? She has overstepped the mark of any propriety in a young lady, and she will not listen to me.'

Rachel took a deep breath and walked over to Alicia.

'Alicia, leave your paints and go straight to your room. Then stay there until I come. I have the staff meeting now so you will have to wait for me. I will not say anything about this outrageous scene and I will get Becky to bring up a tray of tea for you.'

Without looking at Orlando again, Alicia ran from the room and Rachel was left with the art master.

'I am sorry, Rachel, but it is not as it seems. Come and see me off when I go to the station. We can talk then.'

5

After the staff meeting, Rachel waited while Orlando gathered his things together and then walked with him to the front porch. They could talk quietly there. Orlando spoke first.

'What can I say, Rachel, except that I am very sorry? I would say that I did not know that Alicia was still in the room when I was clearing up. I thought that she had left with the other girls, but she suddenly spoke my name and I realised that she was sitting in the window, painting. I ordered her to go straight away, but she did not move. Then I got cross with her and she told me that she was in love with me and started to cry. That was when you came in. I have told you exactly as it happened.'

'Do you love her, Orlando?'

'I adore her. I fell in love with her the

moment I met her and without knowing anything about her. But then we discovered that we talked and thought about painting in the same way, though, of course, Alicia is untutored. But I thought she had it in her to paint well.'

'Does she know that you love her?'

'Good heavens, no. I do know how to behave, especially in a class of young ladies. And in any case, Alicia is planning to marry Mr Knight. I have yet to meet him, but I believe him to be a very worthy gentleman.'

'He is a banker and Alicia's mother does not approve of him.'

'Then even if Alicia cried off, what chance would I have?'

'No chance at all, I should think, unless you eloped with her. Orlando, although Alicia is eighteen years of age, I believe she has been sheltered and in many ways, she is young and innocent. She is also a romantic. She probably thinks that to fall in love with the art master is the most romantic thing she could possibly do. The other thing about Alicia which I have discovered is that she is very wilful. I believe that what is about to happen next, apart from falling in love with you, of course, is that she is going to refuse to start her married life in the lodge of the Old Priory which is Laurence's home. She will insist on him building her a mansion in Bristol.'

'Rachel, you are deliberately showing her at her worst to try and deter me. You will not stop me from loving her, but I have my life and my painting in front of me and if Alicia is promised to Mr Knight, then I must accept it. But what can I do to stop her behaving as she did just now?'

'Mrs Selworthy and I foresaw what would happen and thought that if you made a fuss of all the girls, then Alicia would not be singled out. But you immediately put paid to that by suggesting that she should have individual tuition at the end of your class because you thought she showed promise.'

'I have brought it all on myself. What shall I do?'

Rachel smiled.

'Don't worry, I'll think of something. Fortunately it was me who came into the art room at that moment, so no-one else knows of the situation. I will be able to have a word with Alicia before you come next Friday.'

'Thank you, Rachel. I know I can rely on you. I must go now.'

Rachel watched him hurrying towards the trap and be driven off, then went up to her room thoughtfully. She had to think of what to do next. She decided she must speak to Alicia now, rather than later in the evening. And also believed it would be a good thing to see Laurence, if possible. He had to know the truth.

She knocked on Alicia's door and was glad for once that Alicia didn't share a room as the other girls did. She heard a subdued invitation to enter and in the spacious room which was a bedroom and sitting-room combined, she found a red-eyed, sniffing Alicia sitting on the bed, weeping.

'You will soon lose your beauty if you keep crying like that,' Rachel said.

'You don't know what it means to love someone,' was the reply.

'If I did love someone, I certainly would not behave as you behaved. Mr Ormerod was most embarrassed.'

'He was not,' the girl's words burst out. 'He even wiped my tears and I am sure he loves me even if he didn't say so. Then he was cross with me.'

Rachel sighed. This was going to be more difficult than she had thought.

'Alicia, listen to me, please. I imagine that half your class has fallen in love with the art master, but they all have the sense to keep it to themselves instead of chasing after him as you have done.'

These words seemed to be effective for Alicia looked aghast.

'Miss Biddisham, it didn't seem like

that, did it? I only stayed by the window painting after the others had gone because I had never had the chance of speaking to Orlando privately.'

'And you were foolish enough to tell him that you had fallen in love with him, when he knew very well that you are engaged to Mr Knight.'

'I am all muddled up,' the stricken girl said. 'I do love Laurence and he is very kind to me but it is so different when Orlando is there. It is so thrilling.'

'It is time that you learned that thrills and love are two different things, Alicia. I know that Mr Ormerod is attractive, but he is nice to everyone. He is especially nice to me and I am only the mathematics teacher and not very beautiful either.'

Alicia stared.

'Do you mean that Orlando likes people to admire him?'

Rachel tried not to lose her temper with the foolish girl.

'Mr Ormerod is here as the art master and is very competent. All the work the girls have done has improved in the weeks since he started here. Mr and Mrs Selworthy have both noticed it and they are very pleased. Mr Ormerod is pleasant to them, too,'

She paused and saw that Alicia's face had become serious.

'Be nice to Mr Ormerod if you wish, Alicia, but do not expect your feelings to be returned. Think of Laurence and concentrate on the plans for the wedding. Try and win your mother over, agree to be married from Elford Court and to live at the lodge to start with, even if it is not as grand as the home you have been used to. If you concentrate your energies and thoughts on all those things, you will soon forget Mr Ormerod.'

'Never,' Alicia said. 'But, Miss Biddisham, I knew it would not be a suitable match however much I loved him. So I will try to do as you say.'

Alicia stood up, walked across the room and looked in her mirror. She dabbed her eyes, put a brush to her curls then turned to Rachel.

'I will try to be more like you. I think I am wearing my heart on my sleeve, as the saying goes, and it will not do, will it, Miss Biddisham?'

Rachel gave Alicia a light touch on the shoulder.

'You are learning very quickly, my dear, and please, always remember, if you do need to talk to someone, my room is only just along the landing.'

They left the room together and after Rachel had had some tea, she put on her pelisse. She had made up her mind while she was talking to Alicia that she would walk down to the lodge to seek out Laurence.

It was already dark, but there were light clouds racing across a black moonlit sky. A knock on the door of the lodge brought Mrs Goodwin, Laurence's trusty cook and house-keeper. Rachel had met her before and liked her.

'Why, Miss Biddisham, are you on your own? Do you wish to see the master? I think you will find him in his study.'

Rachel heard herself announced and an exclamation of what seemed like surprised pleasure from Laurence. The study was small, but there was a good fire burning in the grate, which gave the room an appearance of comfort. Laurence had risen from his desk and come forward to meet her.

'Rachel, what a nice surprise. I hope you do not come with bad news.'

He took her hands in his and the touch disturbed them both.

I must be careful, she said to herself. I like him much more than is allowed.

So she smiled at him as he directed her into an armchair near the fire, having helped her off with her pelisse. The room was warm. She spoke calmly in spite of the race of her feelings at his nearness.

'No, it is not bad news, but I felt that you should know what has happened.'

'It is Alicia,' he declared, sitting himself in the chair on the other side of the fireplace. 'She has fallen in love with the art master.'

'How did you know?'

He laughed and his laugh was merry.

'I have seen it coming on these few weeks, but what has the silly girl done now?'

'Laurence,' Rachel said in astonishment, 'you cannot call the young lady you are going to marry a silly girl. What do you mean by it?'

'Rachel, I am very fond of Alicia, but I am of the opinion that she needs to grow up a little. I know that she loves me and that our wedding is already planned, but in many ways, she is still a schoolroom miss. Tell me what she has done now.'

Rachel told him the whole story and he was soon shaking his head.

'Thank you for your help, Rachel, and also for coming to see me. I am grateful. Her parents would be very alarmed to know of her behaviour. I know that Lady Elford does not approve of me, but if she thought that

Alicia might go off with the art master, there would be much grief.'

Rachel looked at him solemnly.

'I told Alicia very much the same, having read her a lecture on the subject of Orlando Ormerod. But I am wondering if a lecture is enough. We know nothing of Mr Ormerod. He might very well be polite and charming to us and he might have produced an excellent reference from the Bristol Art Gallery, but all that does not mean to say that he is not an out-and-out scoundrel who plays with the affections of young ladies wherever he goes. I happen to like him and I get on well with him as a colleague. I think he is a sincere and clever young man, but it doesn't rule out the fact that he is nothing but an itinerant painter who could well be looking for a pretty, young wife amongst his pupils. And Alicia is very rich, you must admit.'

Rachel paused thoughtfully.

'I don't know why I have suddenly thought of all this. I am usually a trusting person and a good judge of character. But then I have never met an artist before! Are you laughing at me, Laurence?'

'No, I am not. I have never met the man, but I would have expected my sister and her husband to have investigated him very thoroughly before making the appointment.'

'Yes, that is true. You are right. I am being unnecessarily suspicious of poor Orlando! I will go back to my original plan. I have thought of something, but I am afraid that you will think it is foolish.'

'I doubt I would ever think of you as foolish, Rachel.'

There was a note in his voice that she had heard before and had wondered about. She must not heed it now.

'I think that the best thing would be to let Alicia see that Orlando is paying attentions to someone else. She would be jealous at first, but she would soon recover and find out how lucky she is to have you.'

'And who would the someone else be?'

'The mathematics teacher,' she said quickly.

Laurence laughed and leaned forward and touched her hand.

'You mean that you would start a flirtation with him? I don't know that I approve. I might be jealous, too.'

Again the enigma and Rachel asked him outright.

'And what is that supposed to mean? Why should you be jealous if I became friendly with the art master?'

'You know nothing of my thoughts, Rachel. I doubt you ever will.'

This time she could not keep back her words.

'You are being very enigmatic and it is not the first time. What are you hiding from me?'

He held the hand he had just lightly touched.

'I am not really hiding anything from you. Some words and feelings are forbidden to me and that is all I will say. But I will promise not to tease you with half-truths. It is a good idea to divert Alicia's attention from Mr Ormerod if you are prepared to do it. Can I leave it to you?'

'Yes. I will think of a ploy and I will have a word with Orlando.'

She laughed.

'There, even I am calling him Orlando! Now I must go.'

She rose to her feet and he stood by her side.

'I will walk down the drive with you. It is after dark though the moon is doing its best to lighten the landscape.'

They walked slowly and Rachel felt strangely in tune with Mr Laurence Knight. Before they reached the house, he pointed to the ruined priory.

'Have you ever seen the ruins by moonlight?' he asked her suddenly.

'I have never seen the ruins at all,' she replied.

'Shame on you. They are worth a visit.'

'I seem to have been too busy and I

always go home on my free day at the weekends,' she told him.

'Would you like me to take you over there? It would be quite romantic.'

'You like to jest, Mr Knight. I think I am having enough trouble with things romantic. But, yes, I would like to go, as long as we are not seen!'

'That would cause a scandal, but we will risk it,' he said playfully.

While they had been talking, Laurence had touched her arm and led her across the grass towards the fallen stones. In minutes, they were standing together, in the shadow of the silvery grey stones whose beauty was enhanced by the moonlight.

'It is very beautiful,' Rachel whispered.

'And so are you.'

'Fiddlesticks,' she replied. 'You tried to flatter me once before. Please do not spoil my pleasure at seeing the ruins for the first time. It seems to be a perfect place for a lovers' tryst.'

She had said the words without

thinking and was startled when he drew her back into a corner where the stone walls had not fallen with the rest.

'Mr Knight,' she said sharply, but her heart was beating hard.

'Miss Biddisham. Shall we pretend we are lovers, just for a moment? Forget about Alicia and her naughty ways. I feel very drawn to you so I will be equally unfaithful.'

Rachel could not move and fought back with her words.

'You choose to behave badly, sir, after letting me think that you were a man of honour.'

'I am a man of honour, Rachel. I would not let Alicia down when I am promised to her. You can believe that it is the moonlight which has struck me, if you like, but I want to kiss you.'

And he pulled her gently towards him and touched her lips with his in what was meant to be a playful gesture. But the playfulness went amiss. Their lips touched and they could not break away. The kiss lingered until Rachel took a step back and stared at him.

'Good heavens, Rachel, I didn't intend passion. You must believe me. It was a kiss in fun, no more. But you have bewitched me and it cannot be. You know that, don't you? I belong to Alicia, for all her faults. Say you will forgive me, please, Rachel.'

Rachel had been glad of his words for they gave her the time to recover. It was her first kiss of passion and she had wanted it to continue. She could have broken away immediately but she had not. Laurence was not the only one who needed to be sorry. She walked a few steps away.

'Laurence, I was just as much at fault. We will forget it. Please, leave me to sit awhile in this lovely place. You go back to the lodge. It is only a few steps for me to walk to the house.'

'Very well, my love. I will hurry back and always have the memory of these sweet moments with you in the ruins.'

Then the serious words changed and his voice became lighter.

'I will leave you to Mr Orlando Ormerod.'

They both gave a chuckle, and Rachel sat and watched as he hurried home. He had called her his love without thinking about it and that she could never be, though she was suddenly startlingly aware that she did love him and had loved him from her first moment of meeting him.

I am just like Alicia, she told herself, then thought of Alicia and gave a groan. I have got to think of a plan to separate Orlando and Alicia. There is only a week and he will be here again.

Even this was not to be, for early the following week, a message came from Bristol to say that Mr Ormerod had an attack of influenza and could not come that Friday, but he hoped to be with them the following week. So passed a smooth week for Rachel, the only interruption to her routine of lessons being a conversation with Sally after her millinery class.

Rachel was glad of the opportunity of

speaking with the young milliner as, over the last few weekends, she had felt a mood of awkwardness in the time spent with Tom Caldicott. She did not see him as often now that she had only the one free day, and, with winter upon them, their walks were limited.

'You should let the girls tidy up for you, Sally,' she said pleasantly as she walked into the room Sally used for her millinery classes.

Sally looked up with a laugh. The two had always dealt well together.

'No, Rachel, I know exactly where each feather and ribbon goes. The girls would be sure to put them in the wrong boxes.'

She stopped and stood looking at Rachel with a sudden strained look.

'Rachel, I have been wanting to speak to you, but I don't quite know how to say it.'

'It is about Tom,' Rachel said.

'Yes, it is about Tom. I will confess that I have always loved Tom but I knew it was hopeless because he had you. But since I started the classes here and he has kindly brought me each early-closing day, and then come to fetch me, we have become very close. Really good friends, I mean, nothing more. I know he wants to speak to me, but he says he can't because he has already asked you to marry him.'

She stopped as though the next words were going to be difficult.

'What shall I do, Rachel? I would like to marry Tom and I am sure he wants to marry me, but . . .'

She could not go on.

'I am standing in the way,' Rachel finished for her.

'Yes,' Sally said simply.

'Sally, I will tell you quite honestly that Tom did ask me to marry him and I turned him down. I did not love him as a woman should love her husband, and now I have met someone else. I know what it is to love someone as you love Tom. Leave it to me. I will see Tom as usual at the weekend and I will tell him the truth. Then when you are here next week, I shall expect an announcement! And if you have a party for your engagement, make sure that it is on my day off and I will be sure to come. Now, actually, Tom will be waiting outside for you. I will go and have a word with him. Then on your way back to Yatton, you can plight your troth, as they say.'

'Thank you, Rachel. I will finish here. Please, tell Tom I won't be long.'

6

On the Friday of the following week, Rachel knew what time Orlando would be brought from the station and she slipped on her pelisse and waited on the steps for him. Rachel knew that she must speak to him before he went into the house.

He jumped down from the trap and joined her with a cheerful smile.

'Hello, Rachel, you look as though you are waiting for me with some purpose in mind.'

'Yes, I am, but I will have to be quick. Are you quite better now?'

'Yes, thank you. I hope that I did not pass it on the last time I was here.'

'No, we are free. The only malady we have is love-sickness.'

'You mean Alicia? It is not something to joke about, you know.'

'Yes, I do know and that is why I am

here,' Rachel replied. 'I have seen Mr Knight and he is of the same opinion as me. If Alicia sees you making a fuss of someone else, we hope that she will soon fall out of love and concentrate on her coming nuptials. She has told me that she still wants to marry Mr Knight even if she loves you for the rest of her life.'

'She is very young,' he said slowly as though to excuse her. 'What is it you have in mind? I can see that you are planning something.'

'Listen carefully then. When your class is finished this afternoon and Alicia leaves the room, I will be there. I am going to send her up to her room to fetch some sketches she did of the other girls. I will come into the art room to speak to you and when Alicia comes back and opens the door, you will move quite close to me as though you have just kissed me, or were just going to kiss me.'

Orlando interrupted quickly.

'Rachel, you would never stoop so

low just to deceive Alicia.'

'Yes, I would. I think she just needs to know that she is not the only girl you admire, and I will deal with her reaction after you have gone. It is not going to do her any harm and I am sorry if you really love her, Orlando, but you must know that it will not do. You did tell me before that you had your career to consider.'

He smiled at her then.

'Do you know, Rachel, you are a remarkable young lady and I admire you. You have Alicia's interests at heart and I must say to myself that it is all for the best. It would not be difficult to kiss you and I will play the charade in the best way I can.'

'Well done,' Rachel said hurriedly. 'You just go in now or they will be thinking that you are not coming again.'

'Very well, I will see you at the end of the day.'

Rachel felt nervous all that day. She finished her last lesson and watched as the girls walked out of the art room. Alicia was almost the last, and when Rachel saw her face, she thought that the girl had a glow about her. Whatever am I doing, Rachel asked herself, but she called out quite calmly.

'Alicia, just a minute. Has Mr Ormerod seen those nice sketches you did of the girls?'

Alicia shook her head.

'No, I did not think they were good enough.'

'But they were excellent. Run and fetch them. He will be pleased. I will go in and tell him that you won't be more than a few minutes.'

She watched as Alicia ran up the stairs, then slipped into the art room. Orlando was frowning.

'We cannot do it, Rachel. The poor child.'

Rachel went up close to him.

'It is for the best. I will tell her afterwards that you are very flirtatious.'

'But I am not. The only person I care about is Alicia,' he protested. 'But I cannot come between her and Laurence Knight.'

Rachel put a hand on his shoulder and smiled at him.

'For heaven's sake, stop scowling and give me a kiss on the cheek.'

He gave a laugh then and the plan worked, for just as he bent to touch her cheek with his lips, the door opened and Alicia stood there.

'Orlando . . . Miss Biddisham . . . oh, how could you!' she wailed.

They heard her running back up the stairs to her room. Rachel took command for Orlando was scowling again.

'Orlando, go to the staff meeting and tell Mrs Selworthy that I have been delayed and will be with you in a few minutes. I will just go and see that Alicia is all right.'

'It is me who is not all right, Rachel,' he said broodingly as she left him.

What a tangle, she thought, as she ran up the stairs. I love Laurence who says he loves Alicia, and Alicia loves

Orlando and he loves her in return. However will it all end?

She knocked on Alicia's door and went in. The girl was standing by the window, staring out at the garden. She glanced round, scowling.

'How could you, Miss Biddisham? I thought you were my friend. You even told me to come to you if I was in trouble.'

Rachel walked up to her.

'Come and sit down. I am afraid that you must understand, Alicia, that your Orlando is something of a ladies' man. I only went in to tell him to wait for you and he was most flattering about me. Before I knew what was happening, he had kissed my cheek, which was very naughty. And he called me beautiful when anyone can see that I have no claim to beauty.'

Alicia was open-eyed and spoke slowly.

'I do believe that you are being truthful with me and I suppose I have been foolish, haven't I? Even if I did love him, I should never have told him so. And you are beautiful, Miss Biddisham. Laurence told me he thought so, at any rate. I can see how silly I have been when I am to marry someone as good as Laurence. Anyone as handsome as Orlando and as dashing, and the art master, is sure to be free with his affections. I promise to be sensible from now on. Now that I can see that you are not upset by Orlando's attentions, I won't take any notice when he flatters me over my painting, and I really will work hard at my mathematics and my painting. That will please Papa, after all.'

She paused and Rachel thought she had spoken sensibly with not too much heartbreak, but there was more to come.

'Even if I love Orlando for the rest of my life,' she said with a show of the dramatic, 'I will never let it show. And I suppose I have been very naïve for we know nothing about him at all. He could be a trickster or a wastrel for all we know. Why are you looking like that?'

Rachel was shaking her head.

'No, it was nothing, Alicia, just something you said that reminded me of Mr Knight.'

She knew that this was only a part truth, for she had been forcibly reminded of her own doubts about Orlando which she had expressed to Laurence, and here was Alicia saying the same kind of thing. She found this surprising and credited the girl with more sense than she had previously shown. Alicia went on speaking.

'Yes, I must be practical and think of Laurence, and one day we will have a fine house in Bristol and lots of children.'

Rachel gave a sigh of relief. It had all turned out well and Alicia was already showing herself to be growing up a little. All will be peaceful in the art room, now, she thought, and hurried downstairs to join the staff meeting.

The next day was a Saturday, but it

was not Rachel's week for going home for the day. She was about to set off for a walk with the girls when Laurence appeared, to see Alicia. She told them to walk on and stopped to have a word with him.

'Rachel, I have come to see Alicia, but I am glad that I have met you first. Did you achieve your plan to try to convince her that Orlando was interested in other young ladies and you in particular?'

She told him what had happened and he was pleased.

'I expect she will tell me all about it in a minute, but I do thank you for your efforts on her behalf.'

He paused and his eyes searched her face.

'Rachel, I have to apologise to you.'

'What do you mean?'

She was genuinely puzzled.

'Have you forgotten the moonlight in the ruins? I am afraid I did not behave as a gentleman should.'

Colour flushed her face at the

memory of the kiss they had exchanged.

'And I did not behave as a lady,' she said hurriedly. 'I have forgotten it already. I spend all my time thinking of Alicia, and Orlando, of course.'

'I would do the same again,' he said soberly.

'And then you would have to apologise all over again. I refuse to listen to you and I must catch up with the girls. And I wish you success with your troublesome fiancée. You will have to be very patient.'

'Yes, I will, Rachel,' he said quickly, 'and I thank you.'

★ ★ ★

Alicia seemed chastened by Orlando's behaviour with Rachel, but as Orlando had promised, he still gave the last half-hour of his Friday lessons to Alicia alone and the conversation was not always on artistic matters. Alicia first of all brought him to task for singling out

Rachel on that afternoon the previous week.

He had set her the task of painting the ruins of the priory from the art room window as it was, by now, too cold to be sitting outside sketching. She paused for a moment in her careful sketch and looked at him.

'Do you admire Miss Biddisham, Mr Ormerod?'

'Yes, I do. I think she is an exceptional person. She is not only nice-looking, but she has the character and intelligence to study mathematics and then to teach the subject.'

'I was jealous when I found you together.'

'Alicia, you must never admit to such sentiment. It does you no credit. It is like me saying I am jealous of Mr Knight because you are engaged to him. As it happens, I have yet to meet him.'

'He is a very good person, but he is not as handsome as you are,' she said and he sighed.

'The proverb goes, Alicia, handsome is as handsome does. Do you understand that?'

'I think so. It is no use looking handsome if your behaviour is not the same,' she answered him. 'But you are a very good person, Mr Ormerod. You cannot deny it.'

'I am not as good as you might think, my dear girl. There is a lot you do not know about me.'

Orlando knew that he was falling deeper and deeper in love with the girl and that he would have to behave very carefully.

'I do not know very much about you. Are you from a local family? But that is a silly question. I would know if you lived near Brompton St Mary. That is where Elford Court is. You have never told me about your family.'

Alicia had started to inquire, but knew that it was something she should not have mentioned, though she thought that she saw an uncomfortable look come into his eyes. There is something of a mystery about him, she said to herself. Surely it cannot be anything bad. I had better try to pass it off lightly. Perhaps it is something he does not wish to talk about.

'Have you any brothers or sisters? I am the only child and I always wanted a brother or a sister.'

Orlando replied rather stiffly.

'My family did not like me becoming an artist and I have very little to do with them.'

Alicia thought he had cleverly avoided her question but made light of it. She gave a little laugh.

'So both of us have displeased our families. My mother does not wish me to marry Laurence. She thinks well enough of him as a person, but you see, he is a banker and she has always expected me to marry higher than that. That is because Papa is a viscount and she is Lady Elford. I think she is a snob.'

'That is not very charitable of you, Alicia. Perhaps she has your interests at heart,' he replied quickly.

'She has only her own interests at heart. I know that it sounds disrespectful of me, but I was brought up to speak the truth.'

She knew that Orlando was regarding her intently.

'I would only say this to you, of course. I feel that I can say what is in my deepest heart to you.'

'I think we have strayed beyond what is permitted in an art class, Alicia, but it has been an interesting conversation and very illuminating. I know now that you are not snobbish, and would marry an artist if he asked you even if your mother disapproved.'

'I would marry an artist if I loved him, and I will say no more, Orlando. There, I have called you by your name and I am not supposed to do so.'

They turned the conversation to the work in hand.

This kind of conversation was continued each Friday until they knew that the break for the Christmas season was going to be hard for both of them.

On top of this, Alicia had another quarrel with Laurence, and this time it was about where they were going to live when they were married. Alicia had hinted before that she did not want to live at the lodge, but Laurence had taken little notice as he knew it to be a small but very lovely house, and he had imagined that Alicia would want to fall in with his wishes. But Alicia was, by now, deeply in love with Orlando and when the quarrel came, it was as though she was looking for an excuse to cry off the engagement.

There was one week left of the term and Alicia was dreading her parting from Orlando on the following Friday. It was the weekend, and on the Sunday, all the girls and the Selworthys walked down the drive into Lymstone to attend morning service.

Alicia knew that she was invited to meet Laurence afterwards and have lunch with him at the lodge. They had done so many times before and it had always been a happy occasion, but on that particular Sunday, Alicia was on edge and Laurence, having just said good morning to a Rachel who looked splendid in her best pelisse and hat, felt that he was going to be out of sympathy with an Alicia who still seemed to yearn for her Orlando.

Mrs Goodwin had the lunch ready for them at the lodge and after they had eaten, Laurence led Alicia into the parlour where a good fire burned in the grate.

'You seem low-spirited today, Alicia,' Laurence remarked as they settled in their armchairs. 'Is there something bothering you?'

She nodded and looked petulant.

'Yes, I don't like this house.'

Laurence showed his astonishment.

'What an extraordinary thing to say. What do you mean by it?'

'I don't want to live in a small house in the country when we are married,' was her reply.

'What do you want then?' he asked, his tone edgy.

'You are a banker, Laurence. Why can't you have a grand house in the city, like the ones in Clifton? I went there once with Papa.'

There is more to this than where we are going to live, he was thinking, but I will let her have her say.

'But I like to think I can get on the train and come back to clear country air. It is very smoky and grimy in the city,' he told her.

'It wouldn't be at Clifton.'

'Alicia, you have hinted before that you did not wish to live here, but I had always thought that if we loved each other, you would be content with anywhere as long as we were together.'

'Do we love each other?'

It was a taunt and came swiftly and not very pleasantly from her, but Laurence knew now what she was about.

'You loved me well enough before Mr Orlando Ormerod appeared on the scene. Has he been forcing his intentions on you?'

Alicia rose angrily.

'Orlando is the perfect gentleman. He gives me extra tuition during the art class and we have had some interesting conversations. There is no more to it than that.'

'I don't believe it.'

Laurence was not easily angered, but that afternoon, he felt like pulling one of the books from the surrounding shelves and throwing it at her.

'You think you are in love with Mr Ormerod and you are trying to force a quarrel between us. But, for heaven's sake, Alicia, can't you be practical for once? Your mother is not best pleased at you marrying a banker. What would she say if you announced that you were going off with a poor artist we know nothing about? Does he live in a garret?'

Laurence knew that he was being nasty, but he suddenly felt completely out of sympathy with Alicia.

'Don't be horrible, Laurence. If you must know, I love Orlando very much and I don't know what I shall do after next Friday. There will be all those weeks at Christmas time when I will not see him.'

'And what about me?' Laurence said angrily.

'If I thought that Orlando would marry me then I would cry off.'

Laurence stared at her. Had he been fooled by her beauty and her pretty ways? Suddenly he saw her as nothing but wilful and selfish. This Orlando Ormerod was welcome to her, he told himself, but he had the feeling that the art master was in no position to support a wife. How could someone who gave lessons at a young ladies' academy once a week afford to have a wife with Alicia's extravagances?

'What are you thinking, Laurence?'

Her voice reminded him that he had been lost in thought.

'I suggest that when you see Mr Ormerod next Friday, you might try to find out if he wishes to marry you. If he does, then I will willingly release you from our engagement.'

'You do not love me. Is it Rachel?'

Oh, no, he thought, however have I had the patience with her all this time? Rachel is a pearl compared to the Honourable Miss Alicia Dunning.

'Rachel is a fine young woman and I believe her to be a very good teacher. My sister has told me so. Rachel also has your interest at heart. I know her to be very concerned for you.'

'You have been talking about me behind my back. It is very cruel of you when we are supposed to be planning our marriage.'

Alicia walked to the door.

'I don't want to stay any longer. I will walk back to the Old Priory by myself.'

'Very well,' Laurence said stiffly. 'I will come and see you next weekend when your parents come to fetch you.'

'I will probably be gone by the time you arrive.'

He stood in the window and watched

her go, and he did not feel in the least guilty that he had not accompanied her. He had never been so out of sympathy with her.

She was so loving when we first met, he told himself. I know she was very young, but I made her wait before we announced our engagement. Now I seem to be seeing her with different eyes. Will she cry off? I do believe it would be a relief to me, but I cannot let her down if the art master fails her. Goodness knows what his intentions are. Surely it will never do.

Just over an hour later, it was at early dusk, he heard a knock on the door. Laurence thought that Alicia must be back to make up their quarrel. But it was Rachel whom Mrs Goodwin showed in.

Laurence rose and took her hands in his. Even before she had time to take off her gloves, he could see that she was troubled.

'Rachel, what is it? You look upset. Is it Alicia?'

She let him help her off with her pelisse.

'Yes, it is Alicia. Whatever has happened? I cannot stop the girl from crying and all she says is that it is Orlando. Has she cried off?'

He sat her down and rubbed her cold fingers.

'You should wear warmer gloves,' he said.

Rachel laughed then, almost glad to do so.

'I come to you with awful problems about Alicia and all you say is that I should wear warmer gloves.'

Laurence laughed, too, and felt a ray of hope as he looked at this wonderful girl.

'Alicia came to you when she got back to the Old Priory?' he asked her.

'Yes, she did. She was in quite a disturbed state and I had to get her some strong tea. Even now I cannot make sense of it all. That is why I have come. Is there anything I can do to help?'

'What did she tell you?' he asked quietly.

'Oh, it all seemed nonsense. She wasn't going to live in the lodge. She would rather live in a garret in Bristol with Orlando. He was a gentleman even if he wouldn't tell her about his family, and she was sure that you, Laurence, didn't love her any more and what would she do if she didn't have Orlando, or you? It went on and on like that until I lost patience with her and walked out and here I am.'

He smiled ruefully.

'Thank you for coming, Rachel. I lost my patience, too. I think I have fallen out of love with Alicia in the space of an hour. I will say no more, but I will not let her down. It seems to me that she is in a state about this Orlando. Maybe she thinks she loves him, but that he doesn't return her love. I would not think very highly of him if he had told her of his love in the middle of a painting lesson. Oh, you can laugh. What is it?' he asked her as he saw her expression change.

'Orlando does love her. He told me so, but I would swear he has not spoken of it to Alicia.'

'Maybe, but whoever he happens to be, he obviously behaves as a gentleman should because he has not taken advantage of the silly girl. Oh, dear, how often have I called her a silly girl? It should have warned me.'

Rachel looked at him seriously.

'But what will you do, Laurence?'

'I must stand by her. She is undergoing some crisis of her own making and I think that the worst part will come on the last day of term when she is parted from him and her parents come to take her back to Elford Court. I will try to be there to see her, if I can get away from the bank a little earlier. Will you be with her, too, Rachel, or will you have gone back to Lymstone?'

'No, I will try to stay until I know she has gone safely home.'

'You are a good person, Rachel. Why

do you trouble yourself so much over Alicia?'

'I am not sure. She is nearly my age, but sometimes she seems so young and defenceless, as though she has not quite grown up. I am sorry, Laurence, it may be your future wife I am talking about.'

'I wish I had my future wife with me now.'

She frowned at him.

'More enigmas, Laurence?'

'Perhaps by Saturday, I may be in a position to explain.'

'What is important about Saturday?' she asked curiously.

'I will know if Alicia is going to cry off or not. But off you go or it will be quite dark and there is no moon in the ruins today.'

These words came from him in a lighter and teasing voice and Rachel was pleased and alarmed at the same time. The memory of the ruins was a dangerous one.

'I think I will come with you, Rachel, and you can go and tell my naughty little girl that I am not going to desert her if she needs me.'

'I will be all right on my own,' she told him. 'It is not quite dark.'

'No, I insist on coming with you, and I might even ask for a kiss.'

'Don't you dare,' she replied with a laugh.

They walked slowly, in pleasant conversation and companionship. Laurence left her as soon as they were through the shrubbery.

'I do want a kiss,' he said.

'I will not allow it.'

'Then I will just take it.'

And he pulled her forward, kissed her briefly and affectionately on the lips and then strode off back to the lodge without another word.

Rachel looked after him, her fingers on lips which had gladly received the kiss. Then she walked slowly into the Old Priory.

7

On the last day of the autumn term at the Old Priory, Rachel woke with a sense of regret. She had enjoyed her first term very much, and she knew she would miss the company of the girls during the Christmas holiday.

Alicia, on the other hand, awoke with a sense of panic. She had quarrelled with Laurence and she was going to have to say goodbye to Orlando for four whole weeks. Not only that, she would miss her last art lesson as the term finished at midday and her parents were coming for her during the afternoon.

At her morning mathematics class, she found that she could hardly concentrate on the theorem which Rachel was explaining to her during her geometry lesson. At the end of it, she rushed along to the art room just in time to catch the younger girls coming out. She breathed a sigh of relief. Orlando had not left. When she went into the room, he turned to her with what seemed to be a happy smile.

'Hello, Alicia, but no lesson today. Have you come to wish me a Happy Christmas? I will miss you.'

The words were spoken with a genuine kindness and carefully hid his true feelings, but they gave Alicia the opening she needed.

'I want to tell you something, Orlando.'

He looked up quickly. He loved this girl who could never be for him and he was quick to notice an urgent note in her voice.

'What is it?' he asked steadily.

'I have quarrelled with Laurence. I am not going to marry him.'

He put out a hand towards her, then drew back.

'You have cried off?'

'Yes.'

She knew it was not the exact truth, but it would be so within the hour when Laurence and her parents arrived.

'Would you like to tell me why?'

He was now standing very close and looking down at her. Alicia took a deep breath. She was determined to say it.

'I cannot marry Laurence when I love someone else.'

Their eyes met and he knew her meaning only too well.

'You love me?'

He said it so quickly that she could hardly hear the words.

'Yes, I do. I tried not to love you. I tried hard to do what Laurence wished, but it was no good, and when I found you with Miss Biddisham, it made no difference though I pretended to myself that you were making a fuss of her just as you did all the others.'

'All the others, Alicia?' he asked.

'Well, Miss Biddisham then.'

'And what if I tell you that Miss Biddisham means nothing to me and that I believe her to be in love with your Laurence? What would you say then?'

'I, too, have suspected Laurence and

Miss Biddisham. It would be nice,' she answered him almost eagerly.

Orlando smiled. This sweet child was so innocent, and he felt very protective towards her.

'So it means that it could be Laurence and Rachel, and you and me? Would you like it to be you and me, Alicia?'

'Yes,' she whispered, 'I would, Orlando, and I do love you.'

'And do you suppose that I love you?'

'Yes, I think so. It was the way we felt when we first met, and then, later on, we got on so well during the art lessons.'

Orlando now knew that he had somehow to protect this girl he loved. It would be for the rest of his life, but how was it to be accomplished? She knew nothing of his background and there were certain things about himself he would have to explain to her, but he did not wish to commit himself until he was absolutely certain of her feelings.

'Listen, Alicia,' he said softly, 'I love

145

you very much, but I am only an artist and your parents would never permit you to marry me. How can I ask you to be my wife?'

'I told Miss Biddisham that I would rather live in a garret with you than to be married to Laurence when I loved you all the time.'

He was startled.

'Alicia! I would not ask you to marry me if I lived in a garret. I have a perfectly respectable house in Bristol. It belongs to my father.'

She stared at him.

'Your father? You have never spoken of your family, even when I asked you, though you did tell me that they disapproved of you being an artist.'

He put his hands on her shoulders to steady both of them.

'Let me think, Alicia, and you must think, too. It is no use suggesting that we elope because I will not be party to such an exploit. But I will say this.'

He bent and kissed her cheek.

'That is all I will allow myself. It

seems that we do love each other and so I will ask you properly. Will you marry me, Alicia?'

Her eyes were shining and she looked prettier than ever.

'Oh, Orlando, thank you, thank you. Yes, please, I will marry you. I would run off in the middle of the night with you if necessary.'

'Calm down, calm down, for that will not be necessary for I have thought of a solution. Your parents will never approve of me, but I think that mine would like you very much. Will you let me take you to them and I will obtain a licence and we can be married in a few days' time?'

Alicia had her first doubts. She had never done anything without her parents' permission.

'Do you think it would be proper, Orlando?'

Orlando had not told her the whole truth for reasons of his own, but he was convinced that it was the only way to secure Alicia as his wife. That meant more to him than anything else in the world, except perhaps his painting. He would not give that up even for Alicia, but there should be no need. He spoke firmly to her.

'I will make it proper, my sweet. This is the plan. Your parents are coming for you this afternoon. Go home with them to Elford Court and tomorrow morning, be at the gates near your lodge and I will bring a carriage for you. Have a bag packed with whatever you will need. I will take you straight to my parents' home and you can send a message to your mama from there. Will you do that?'

'It will be like an elopement,' she told him, 'but not a proper elopement. Do your parents live far away, Orlando?'

'Not too far and it is possible that my father might be known to yours.'

'That seems strange,' she said with a little frown.

'Don't worry your pretty little head about it, but do just as I say. I am going to leave you now so that I can go and make all the arrangements. I will say goodbye until tomorrow morning, but I am not going to kiss you yet. We will have a lifetime of kisses before us.'

'Oh, Orlando.'

And Mr Ormerod, art master, picked up his case and left the room. Alicia looked after him and did not know in her heart if he was a hero or a rogue. Whichever he is, I love him, she told herself and prepared to meet her parents. She knew that it was wicked to run off with Orlando, but if it was the only way to secure his love, she would look forward to it with a sense of adventure. Orlando seemed to be keeping something from her, but she trusted him and did not believe that he would treat her badly.

That afternoon, Laurence arrived before Lord and Lady Elford. He found Alicia with her cases and bags packed and waiting in the drawing-room. Most of the girls had already left.

Alicia is looking defiant, Laurence thought. She cannot hide her feelings.

'Well, Alicia, are you going to cry off?'

He thought to give her the opening. She chose to be gracious.

'I am sorry if I am letting you down, Laurence, but it is Orlando I love. It would not be fair to go through a pretence of marriage with you.'

'And has Mr Ormerod asked you to marry him?'

'He has,' came the pert reply.

Good heavens, he thought, whatever are her parents going to say to that? I suppose she has the Christmas break to prepare them for the news.

'I willingly release you from our engagement, Alicia, and wish you every happiness,' he stated formally.

'Don't you want to know what our plans are?' she asked him.

'Not particularly,' he replied curtly.

'Orlando has a substantial residence in Bristol.'

Laurence laughed to himself.

'I have no doubt it will suit you better than the lodge of the Old Priory.'

He knew he was being ungenerous, but was stopped from saying anything further by the entrance of Rachel.

'Alicia, your parents are here. Are you ready?'

Rachel looked at the girl and could discern a sense of triumph about her. She has cried off from marrying Laurence, she guessed, and Orlando has told her that he loves her. That the wilful girl has made further plans, she did not begin to imagine.

'Miss Biddisham, I must tell you that Laurence and I are no longer engaged to be married,' Alicia announced quite proudly.

Rachel looked quickly at Laurence. Their eyes met with meaning and he gave a slight grin.

'Alicia . . . '

But he was not allowed to finish for Lord and Lady Elford had followed Rachel into the room. Introductions were made.

'Papa, Mama, this is Miss Biddisham, my mathematics teacher, and,

Mama, I am not going to marry Laurence after all.'

Rachel watched the pantomime which followed. Lady Elford was a large woman and not handsome. She was dressed in voluminous furs and her hat also had fur around it. Her voice boomed.

'Thank goodness you have seen sense at last, Alicia,' she said to her daughter but looked around to them all. 'Mr Knight, I have nothing against you, but I did not approve of my daughter marrying a banker. It would have been quite beneath a Dunning to have married someone who worked in the city. Maybe if you had been knighted, it would have been a different matter.'

Rachel almost froze at this speech and could suddenly understand the free spirit of Alicia rebelling against her mother. Thankfully, she soon found that Lord Elford was a gentleman of much more reasonable sense and manner. He came over to her and shook her by the hand.

'Miss Biddisham, you have my admiration and my gratitude. If you have been able to teach this harum-scarum daughter of mine the principles of mathematics, I consider that you must be a genius, and I do know that she values your friendship. I thank you.' Then he added very quickly, 'I had no objection to you, Mr Knight, but I let my wife have her way for a quiet life.'

Rachel liked him as much as she disliked the forbidding Lady Elford. When they had gone, taking a radiant Alicia with them, Rachel found Laurence by her side.

'I am free,' he told her.

'Are you pleased? You do not seem to be upset at Alicia crying off.'

'No, I am relieved in a way. I was misled into believing that her character was as beautiful as her looks, and I have to say that I think that your Mr Ormerod must have told her that he loves her. She looks like the cat who has stolen the cream!'

Rachel laughed.

'Yes, I thought the same. But surely she cannot imagine that he will marry her. And what would Lady Elford have to say to that? She is rather a gorgon, is she not?'

'Gorgon is a good word. I am not sure whose interests she has at heart, Alicia's or her own. But let us forget about the Elfords for a moment to think about us. Don't look so surprised, Rachel. Will you give me permission to call upon you in Lymstone on one fine weekend during the holiday?'

Rachel felt a glow, not only of pleasure but of hope.

'It would be very nice, Laurence, thank you.'

But it was to be less than twenty-four hours before Laurence and Rachel were to meet again.

The next day, Rachel was up early and helping her father in the post office when, just before mid-day, she was astonished when Laurence walked in — and it was a Laurence who looked unusually agitated.

'Laurence, what is it? Come into the parlour. We can be private there.'

He did not delay, nor would he sit down.

'Rachel, I need your help. It is very urgent. I have just received a message from Elford Court. Read that.'

He held out a piece of paper to her.

She took it and saw that it was a very few words and written in a large, hasty scrawl. She read it aloud.

'Dear Mr Knight, we need your help. Alicia has eloped with the art master. Can you come and please bring the mathematics teacher with you for we will need her? Bertha Dunning, Lady Elford.'

Rachel shook her head and read it again to herself, finding it hard to believe. When she looked up at Laurence, his expression was very serious.

'I cannot believe that Orlando would elope with the girl, but, Laurence, they must have planned it yesterday. That was why Alicia was looking so cock-a-hoop when she left. Oh, my goodness me, the silly, silly girl. She knew that her mother would never accept Orlando. Will you go, Laurence?'

'Yes, I must. I still have a fondness for the girl even if I have fallen out of love with her. As she has said before, we know nothing of this Ormerod. He may be the greatest blackguard of all time. Will you come with me, Rachel?'

'Yes, of course I will come. Just let me tell Papa and fetch my pelisse.'

It was an easy ride to Brompton St Mary and the lanes were reasonably dry. At Elford Court, they were received with much to-do by Lady Elford who launched into a lengthy tirade at once.

'Thank you for coming, Laurence, and you, too, Miss Biddisham. We are in a great sense of shock. I will get Alicia's note to show you. Who is this art master? All we know about him is that he was struck with Alicia's talent and gave her special tuition. One wonders now at his motives. He sounds like a rogue to me. Whatever are we going to do? I hope you will be able to suggest something, Laurence, and . . . '

She is never going to stop talking, Rachel thought, but the note was given to Laurence who then passed it to Rachel.

Dear Mama, she read, *This is to let you know that I have eloped with Orlando. We do love each other and he is taking me to his house which is somewhere in Bristol. Do not worry about me, I am very happy.*

With fondest love, Alicia.

Rachel shook her head, then looked at Lady Elford. She felt almost sorry for the irate woman who had dispensed with a banker as a prospective son-in-law only to acquire a penniless artist. It was then that Lord Elford spoke. He addressed himself to Laurence.

'Is it possible to find out where the young man lives in Bristol?'

'I think he does live in Bristol,' Laurence replied carefully, 'but not with his family.'

'It may not be as bad as we think,'

Rachel said. 'It does look as though he has had the decency to take her to his parents' home. What do you think, Laurence?'

Laurence turned to Alicia's father.

'Lord Elford, my sister and her husband will know of Ormerod's direction. Would you like Miss Biddisham and me to drive back to the Old Priory and try to locate the pair of them? What is it, Rachel?'

He stopped as Rachel put her hand on his arm to try and stop him.

'Laurence,' she said, 'Mr and Mrs Selworthy have gone up to London on a visit. I believe they left early this morning.'

He frowned.

'Yes, you are right. I had quite forgotten in the to-do over Alicia. I said goodbye to them last night. Then I think that the next best thing would be to go to the Art Gallery in Bristol. Mr Ormerod spends some of his time working there. What do you think, Lord Elford?'

Lord Elford was not given the chance to reply for Lady Elford was giving Laurence a smile.

'Would you do that? I would be most grateful for I really do not know where to turn. The only thing I could think of was to send for you, Laurence, and to think I considered you were not good enough for my daughter.'

Laurence and Rachel rose quickly. They went straight to the stables for their trap. Their worries would have been eased somewhat if they had been aware of the actual progress of Alicia and Orlando.

Alicia had been waiting that morning as she had been told to do, but she was feeling both agitated and nervous. When Orlando arrived, he was in a carriage driven by a coachman. This did nothing to soothe Alicia's nerves as she wondered what the impoverished artist was doing in a splendid carriage, but as the coachman stowed away her case and Orlando helped her in, she had the thought that at least she would not be seen driving away.

She sat close to Orlando as they were driven along and held her hands tightly together under her muff. Then she felt a tear trickle down her cheek and had to raise a hand to brush it away quickly.

'What is it, my love?' Orlando asked kindly.

He had expected hysterics and knew what he was going to do.

'Stop the carriage, Orlando, I can't do it. I do love you and I would live with you in a garret, but it is a disgrace for poor Mama and Papa. I should not have agreed to elope with you.'

She paused and looked out of the small window at passing fields.

'Where are we and why have you suddenly got a carriage and a coachman? I was waiting for you to come in a trap. Are you abducting me?'

'We are on our way to my parents as I promised you. I am sure that they will welcome you kindly when they see how beautiful you are.'

'It is no use being beautiful,' she

cried out with a sob. 'Everyone expects me to behave beautifully, too, and I am selfish and vain and wilful, and I can be quarrelsome, too. Tell the coachman to turn back, Orlando. I cannot let Papa down by eloping with you. I don't mind about Mama because she was horrid to Laurence. Are you going to do as I ask?'

'I don't think so, Alicia,' he replied calmly.

'What do you mean?'

'You are going to do as I say, and if you do indeed love me, I shall expect obedience from you.'

Orlando knew what lay ahead and was certain of the outcome. For all her admitted faults, he did love Alicia.

'But I won't do as you say. It is not proper for me to be here on my own with you. I should never have agreed to it in the first place. I am bringing shame on the family.'

Orlando was unmoved and had taken hold of her hands.

'You look lovely when you are angry, Alicia. Will you let me kiss you? We are in a closed carriage and no-one will see us.'

'Let me out! You are not a gentleman, you are a common artist, an upstart, a braggart. I hate you for doing this to me.'

'And I love you. I won't ask you for a kiss, I will take it.'

And with these words, he found her lips. He had wanted to kiss her so many times before, but they had never been on their own at the Old Priory.

Alicia, angry and uncertain all at the same time, felt passion for the first time in her young life. The kiss was a gentle affair and when it had finished, she hid her head against him and sobbed.

'I should not have let you kiss me, Orlando, and yet I wanted you to. I even enjoyed it.'

Orlando roared with laughter and she looked at him in astonishment.

'If you are going to say things like that when we are married, we can expect an enjoyable time. Now, I am going to be serious. Do you trust me?'

'I don't know. I want to, but I would like to know where you are taking me. I can see that we have not entered Bristol yet. How can I trust you?'

'Just listen to me for a moment and I will try to explain. Let me tidy your hair and put your hat on again. It is a very fetching hat, by the way. Then you will sit still and I will hold your hand and in ten minutes we will be at my home. My parents will adore you. They have been waiting for me to find the young lady who would make me happy for the rest of my life.'

'But you told me that you had displeased your parents.'

'Yes, I know, but it was only because I insisted on becoming an artist when they wanted me to go into parliament or enter the church.'

'I must be truthful, Orlando, and say I cannot imagine you as a vicar. So they did not like it when you became an artist. Do you think I will like them?'

She asked the question and felt herself become nervous again.

'I think you will have a surprise.'

'I see. You are determined to tell me nothing.'

She looked out of the window.

'We are going through a village. Are we nearly in Bristol?

'No, but we are nearly there.'

He spoke both cheerfully and calmly and Alicia held on to his hand tightly. Suddenly, she knew that she could trust him and that she must prepare herself to meet his parents, whoever they might be.

8

It was a good road into Bristol from Brompton St Mary and Laurence and Rachel found themselves in the city well before lunch time. They stopped at a hotel for a quick luncheon before making their way along College Green, past the cathedral, and then up Park Street to the Museum and Art Gallery, an imposing building at the top of the hill.

It looked locked up and deserted, but leaving the trap in the forecourt, Laurence walked up to the main door and rang the bell. Rachel heard the bell jangling as though it was in an empty building. However, the door was opened and a gentleman, who looked to be dressed in the suit of an official, asked them quite pleasantly what it was they wanted. There was no-one working in the gallery, it being a

Saturday, he told them.

'We are looking for Mr Orlando Ormerod,' Laurence said politely. 'I understand that he sometimes works here.'

'Young Mr Ormerod? Yes, certainly he does, except on a Friday when he travels out to Yatton to teach at a young ladies' academy. Might I know who is asking for him?

The man did not look at them suspiciously, but he had spoken with care.

'I am Mr Laurence Knight, banker, of Bristol and this is Miss Biddisham, who is a teacher at the academy. Mrs Selworthy, who owns the Old Priory together with her husband, is my sister. We are anxious to see Mr Ormerod. Mr and Mrs Selworthy are away so we cannot ask them his direction.'

'I see, that sounds satisfactory, but I do not know that I am going to be of any help. All I know about Mr Ormerod is that he has a studio above a shop in

Whiteladies Road. It is above Hoopers, the linen-drapers.'

Laurence replied to the helpful official.

'Thank you very much. That is indeed most helpful. I believe Whiteladies Road to be just up the road beyond Queens Road.'

'That is correct, sir. I hope you succeed in finding Mr Ormerod at home.'

Back in the trap, Rachel was laughing with delight.

'Laurence, Orlando does live in a garret. Would he take Alicia there?'

'I hope not, Rachel,' he replied and she thought he sounded grim.

They found the linen-drapers easily and it was open and busy. They asked for Mr Hooper and a short, neat man came hurrying from an office behind the counter.

'Mr Ormerod? Yes, he has the attic rooms as a studio. He says the light is good. No, I do not believe he is here today, but if you will wait a moment, I will send one of my assistants up to see.'

They watched as a young man was sent on the errand and Mr Hooper turned back to them. The draper was most polite and keen to be helpful.

'Mr Ormerod does not live here, but I expect you know that. The two attic rooms were knocked into one space and a roof-light put in. He works some of the time at the Art Gallery and one day a week he teaches art at an academy out Yatton way.'

Rachel found herself lost for words and was glad when Laurence asked the question she was trying to phrase in her mind.

'Do you know where Mr Ormerod actually lives, Mr Hooper?'

'Why, yes,' the helpful little draper replied. 'It is called Groome House, in Ashleigh Avenue. It is just off the Queens Road. I do not know if he just has rooms there or if he lives with his family, but that is where you will find him. Ah, here is Robert. There was no-one there? Thank you for going up.'

He turned back to Laurence and Rachel.

'I hope that I have been of some help, sir. Good-day and I trust you will find Mr Ormerod at home.'

Laurence and Rachel sat in the trap and looked at each other.

'This is nothing but a wild-goose chase,' Laurence said. 'Do you suppose there is some mystery about Mr Orlando Ormerod?'

Rachel laughed.

'I suppose it is all quite possible. Are we going to try to find Groome House?'

'I think we must do. A turning off Queens Road? It should not be difficult to find. Ah, here we are, Ashleigh Avenue. Why, it is a road of rather grand houses. This is unexpected. They are in the Georgian style, very imposing. Do they have names?'

'Yes, there is Ashleigh House and Hampton Villa . . . oh, here it is, Laurence, Groome House. They all have short drives at the entrance. What are we to expect? It is hardly the type of house to give lodgings to an impecunious artist.'

'We will enquire, Rachel.'

The door was opened by a liveried footman.

'Sir? Madam?' he said.

'We are hoping to find Mr Orlando Ormerod here. He was not at the art gallery or at the studio.'

'Mr Orlando, sir? May I ask who is seeking him?'

Laurence told the same tale and the politeness of the footman turned to friendliness.

'Do come into the drawing-room. Mr Orlando has gone over to Groome Castle today, and it was very early this morning, scarcely light. It seemed to be a very special occasion. He was very busy packing last night and seemed happy. I must say that it is a long time since he has seen his parents, but he paid them a visit yesterday afternoon before coming home.'

Rachel looked at Laurence and

Laurence looked at Rachel. They were both of them utterly bewildered.

'You look puzzled, sir, if I may say so,' the footman said. 'Yet you appear to know Mr Orlando quite well, especially Miss Biddisham if she is also a teacher at the academy. Mr Orlando does enjoy teaching the young ladies each week, for he has told me so.'

Rachel was forced to speak, for Laurence seemed to be struck dumb.

'Do you think you could tell us who Mr Ormerod's parents are? You see, he has never spoken of his family to us.'

'Well, bless my soul, but I am not surprised seeing that Lord Beckington did not approve of Mr Orlando becoming an artist.'

'Lord Beckington?' Rachel echoed.

'Yes. Mr Orlando's parents are Lord and Lady Beckington of Groome Castle at Chewton Mendip. Oh, I can see that I have surprised you. Was the naughty boy pretending to be a penniless artist? I have known him since he rode his first pony, you know.'

Laurence and Rachel looked at each other and burst out laughing, then had to apologise to the footman and try to explain the situation.

'The Honourable Miss Dunning and daughter of Lord and Lady Elford? Well, how very nice, indeed it is,' the footman said. 'No, Mr Orlando would never have eloped with the young lady. He will be taking her safely to Groome Castle, you mark my words. And Lord and Lady Beckington will be pleased. They have been wanting a suitable match for him. Must you go now? But please let me offer you some refreshment,' he added as Laurence and Rachel made to leave.

Laurence shook his head.

'Thank you very much, but we must be on our way back to Elford Court and we did already stop for luncheon.'

'Very well. I'm glad to have met you and tell Mr Orlando when you find him that James is very pleased.'

Out in the trap once more, Laurence put his arms around Rachel and she put her head against his chest and laughed and laughed.

'What next?' she said.

'I think we have just got time to get back to Elford Court before it gets dark. Lady Elford is going to be pleased, is she not? Lord Beckington is an earl, I believe.'

He put his cheek against hers for a second.

'Then tomorrow morning, I think perhaps we will travel on to Chewton Mendip to find out what Orlando and Alicia are up to!'

At about the same time as Rachel and Laurence had entered Bristol, the carriage carrying the eloping pair drew up outside the magnificent Groome Castle, on the edge of the Mendip Hills in Somersetshire. As she was helped down from the carriage, the Honourable Miss Alicia Dunning stared at Orlando in disbelief.

'Where are we?' she asked him in complete bewilderment. 'This is not Bristol.'

'This is Groome Castle, my home.'

'But Groome Castle is the home of the Earl of Beckington. Papa knows that.'

'That is right, my love. Thomas George Ormerod, fourth Earl of Beckington, is my father.'

'You are the son of the Earl of Beckington? You have been fooling me all this time, letting me think that you were a penniless artist?'

He took her arm gently.

'I am a younger son, Alicia, and I am virtually penniless. I am also an artist. I have told you no untruths.'

'But why . . .'

He guided her towards the front door which made the portico of the Old Priory look tiny.

'No questions now. I will answer them all later. First, come and meet my parents. They are expecting you, but I will tell you first that they do not know of the elopement plan, just that I wish to marry you and have brought you to meet them.'

A footman stood at the door, an elderly man who smiled broadly when he saw who it was.

'You have made good time, Master Orlando. The earl and countess are in the blue drawing-room. They are expecting you.'

By this time, Alicia was speechless and overcome with awe. She had always been accustomed to good living and a fine house, but nothing she had ever known approached the grandeur of Groome Castle. And what about Orlando's father and mother? She put her hand into Orlando's and held it tight.

Inside the magnificent drawing-room sat two people. They rose as soon as Orlando and Alicia entered the room, and Alicia's reaction on seeing them was to smile.

Lord Beckington was not tall, but his hair was still dark and he was handsome. Alicia could see that Orlando had got his looks from his father, until her gaze passed to the countess. Lady

Beckington was short, plump, but she was also dark-haired and at the age of nearly fifty years, she could still be described as a very lovely woman.

Orlando went up to her and kissed her.

'Mama, may I present to you the Honourable Miss Alicia Dunning, only daughter of Lord and Lady Elford of Elford Court. Alicia, this is my dear mama.'

Alicia stepped forward shakily. She put out her hand to have it taken in warm fingers which seemed to give a welcome of their own.

'My dear girl, I am very pleased to meet you and you are just as beautiful as Orlando said you were. The naughty boy, he has not been to see us since he started teaching at the academy and yesterday he arrives to tell us that he has fallen in love with the most beautiful girl he has ever seen, and also that he would like to bring you to meet us. And here you are. Now you must meet the earl. Thomas, dear, this is

Alicia. You will admit to her being very pretty indeed.'

The Earl of Beckington shook hands with Alicia, smiled at her and then looked towards his wife, saying, 'Just as pretty as you were when we met over thirty years ago, my dear.'

Then he turned back to Alicia.

'Now come along and sit with us and we will try to recommend our son to you. He is not the heir, you know. That is our eldest son, William, Lord Groome, who lives not so far away from us on his own estate at Compton Martin. But Orlando will receive a portion on his marriage and I have suggested to him that he shows you the West Wing of Groome Castle with a view to making it your home. It needs a lot of attention, but you would be free to choose the decoration and furniture of your choice. We did not approve of Orlando being an artist, I expect he has told you so, but he has done well and could make himself a studio here if he wished to do.

'He is living in our town house in Bristol at the moment and, of course, he would still have the use of it after his marriage. Now, my wife is looking at me. Am I saying too much? I certainly approve of my son's choice of bride and would like to meet Lord and Lady Elford. I do seem to remember, my dear girl, that your father and I met at the races at Newmarket in our youth.'

He looked at the countess.

'What do you say to having the Elford family here to luncheon tomorrow? I am suggesting luncheon because it is too dark to be journeying about the countryside after dinner.'

'A splendid idea,' Lady Beckington replied. 'What do you say to that, Alicia?'

Orlando had been standing back, smiling, while this conversation had been going on. Now he wanted Alicia to speak and she did not let him down.

'Lady Beckington, Lord Beckington, it is a great honour to meet you and to come to this lovely house. I will confess to having fallen in love with Orlando the moment I met him and now I have discovered that he felt the same for me. I love him dearly and will be a good wife, and I am sure we will be very happy to live here.'

Orlando stepped forward and put a hand on her shoulder.

'Bless you, Alicia,' he said. 'We will have luncheon here and I will show you round. Then I will take you back to Elford Court to ask your father formally for your hand in marriage. We seem to have got it the wrong way round and I should have asked him first, but I am sure it will all be agreed upon quite happily. Come and walk over to the West Wing with me.'

As Alicia walked down endless, carpeted corridors, she felt that she was beginning to breathe and think again after the shock of her arrival at Groome Castle. Orlando opened a door into a large room with very little furniture, and what there was covered with holland covers.

'I think this would make a good drawing-room,' he began to say when he was confronted by a whirlwind of an Alicia.

She stood in front of him and banged her fists against his chest.

'You did not tell me! You let me think that you were Mr Ormerod, the art master. You let me have the shock of arriving here at this beautiful place which is your home, and meeting the lovely people who are your parents. How could you do it? How could you let me think we were eloping, even when I realised the enormity of it once we were in the carriage? How could you do it?' she repeated.

His reply was to hug her closely to him and then kiss her thoroughly until she could not stop herself from returning the kiss.

'Alicia, you will have to try and understand and forgive me. I have lived the life of an artist for nearly five years. Father at last agreed to send me to the Slade School and then I established

180

myself at the Bristol Art Gallery and found myself a studio. I came home very rarely. I don't need to tell you what happened next. I applied for the post of art master at the academy. It somehow pleased me to be able to teach. That is how I met you, and you know what happened then.'

'We fell in love,' she said and kissed his cheek shyly. 'But still you did not tell me. You told no-one, in fact.'

'No, I really was Mr Ormerod, the art master, and I was not faced with a decision until yesterday. You forced it on me, you little minx. And you must remember, Alicia, that all the time I was there that you were still engaged to Laurence. I could not even have any hopes.'

'But it was you I loved, not Laurence. I know that now.'

'Yes, I know you do and now you realise that we are in a bit of a quandary with coming to my parents first,' he said suddenly serious.

'I suppose we are. I left a note for

Mama telling her that I was eloping with you.'

'Did you use the word elope?'

She nodded.

'Yes, but I did say that we were going to your house in Bristol.'

'Your mama will be worried. She will be beside herself with worry. I think we must have a very quick luncheon and be back there as soon as possible. Do you suppose your mama will approve of this match?'

Alicia grinned.

'She will be beside herself with joy, her daughter married to the son of an earl. You have yet to meet my mama and I think she will compare very unfavourably with your sweet mother, who was so kind to me.'

They took a quick look around the West Wing and were very satisfied. Then they hurried back into the house for luncheon.

After lunch, they travelled back to Elford Court only to arrive there at the same time as Laurence and Rachel returning from Bristol! Inside the big house, there was mayhem. Laurence was introduced to Orlando and Laurence related the story of the chase round Bristol after the eloping pair. Orlando was amused and most apologetic and the two young gentlemen found that they had a lot to say to each other.

Rachel and Alicia were talking, crying and laughing at the same time and Lady Elford was quite overcome. She and Lord Elford were found in the drawing-room and it was immediately obvious that Alicia's mama had been weeping. She looked up when the four young people entered the room and she cried out loud.

'Oh, Laurence, thank you! You have found them. Alicia.'

She rose to take Alicia in her arms.

'You wicked girl. How could you do it to me? And this is the art master? How dare you elope with my daughter, young man. What is it, Alicia?'

'Mama and Papa, you must let me

introduce Orlando to you. This is Orlando Ormerod, the younger son of the Earl of Beckington of Groome Castle. No, you have no need to stare at me. It is quite true and I have only discovered it myself today. Orlando took me to his parents at Groome Castle and we did not elope after all. Orlando, you tell them. They will listen to you.'

Orlando made a polite bow to Lady Elford and shook hands with Alicia's father.

'I am sorry to have caused you so much distress. I had no idea until later that Alicia had left you a note saying she had eloped with me. We did not elope and it was never my intention. I took Alicia straight to my parents this morning. I must tell you that Alicia has known me only as Mr Ormerod and that at the Old Priory, no-one knew of my connections.'

He turned and grinned to Laurence.

'Though it does look as though Laurence and Rachel succeeded in tracking me down, as they will tell you in due course. As to my family, I am a younger son and had to make my own way. I refused to go into the church or into parliament, so my good father sent me to art school and I have been successful.'

He turned to Lord Elford.

'I am sorry, sir, that we have caused you some alarm this morning and now respectfully ask your permission to make my addresses to Alicia. I love her very much. Oh, and my father thinks he might have met you at Newmarket in days gone by.'

Lord Elford could only smile and he shook hands with Orlando again.

'I welcome you as a son-in-law, Ormerod, and hope that you will be able to convince my wife of your prospects as a husband for our only daughter. And it looks as though you know how to handle the pretty little madam. I am afraid we have spoiled her. It was just like Alicia to want to elope, but you had the decency to take her straight to your parents. I appreciate that and can only hope that they approve of her.'

Orlando smiled and immediately replied, 'They are delighted and have offered us the West Wing of Groome Castle. I think Lady Elford will be pleased.'

Lady Elford was very pleased indeed and they all thought that she would never stop talking. She turned to Orlando.

'And to think that Alicia is going to live in Groome Castle. You will be too grand for us. And Mr Ormerod — no, I am going to call you Orlando as Alicia does — I know that you will take care of our little girl. And to think she is going to marry the son of an earl! I could not have asked for better. I must explain that I had no objection to the manners and characters of Mr Laurence Knight, but he was only a banker, after all. I think he must feel pleased not to have our troublesome daughter on his hands. And what do you say? You think he will marry Miss Biddisham? It does rather look that way to see the two of them together. I am pleased. She has been a good friend to Alicia.

'And now I must tell you, Orlando, that you are as handsome as everyone made you out to be and it will be a feather in my cap to have you as a son-in-law. You are not taking our daughter far away and I trust that you will invite us to the West Wing of Groome Castle. Give me a kiss, Alicia, and I will forgive you the scare you gave me this morning, telling us that you had eloped. I will invite you to take dinner with us, Orlando. Laurence, will you and Miss Biddisham stay, too? We have to thank you for all your efforts to find Orlando in Bristol. You will not stay? No, I quite understand and I wish you every happiness if it is not too premature.'

Rachel managed to say goodbye to Alicia, and Laurence had a few words with Orlando, then they crept away.

'Laurence, it is nearly dark,' Rachel whispered as they got outside.

'I have my lanterns and I know the road very well. I am taking you back to the Old Priory, Rachel, for I shall have something to say to you when we reach the ruins.'

'Laurence,' Rachel said with an air of mischief in her voice, 'I hope it is something I wish to hear.'

He helped her up into the trap and they sat closely for the few miles back to the Old Priory. They could not stop talking and Rachel was laughing, too. This was a new Laurence she was seeing.

'You sound very carefree all of a sudden,' she told him.

He smiled.

'Do you know, Rachel, that is a very good way of putting it? Yes, I think I have been burdened with the care of Alicia for some time and now Orlando has taken her away from me. They seem very happy, but I am free from having to dissuade her from wanting to marry from the Old Priory instead of from her home, free from trying to persuade her to live at the lodge, and free from having that dreadful woman as a mother-in-law! So, yes, I am free, Rachel. I can enjoy the drive back to the Old Priory with you at my side and I can say what I have been wanting to say when we get there. I believe that Lady Elford is going to be delighted with Orlando, don't you? I liked him very much. He has got Alicia's measure and I think they will be happy.'

He paused to look down at her as they swung round into the drive of the Old Priory.

'No moon tonight, Rachel.'

'Did you want a moon?' she asked light-heartedly.

'Yes, I feel romantic. I hope you do, too.'

'I'll think about it,' she replied and felt a great happiness at what she knew was to come.

They walked to the ruins hand in hand. Rachel felt cold and said so.

'Come and sit on the stones and I will keep you warm.'

They sat together and he enfolded her in a loving embrace.

'Three questions, my love,' he said softly.

'Whatever do you mean?'

'Please, will you marry me, because I love you very much? Will you mind living at the lodge when we are married? And lastly, please may I kiss you?'

'The answer is yes, to all three, Laurence.'

'Is that all you are going to say?'

She smiled in the dim light.

'And I love you very much.'

The long kiss that followed was a happy affair and a happy conclusion to all their troubles.

THE END

We do hope that you have enjoyed reading this large print book.

Did you know that all of our titles are available for purchase?

We publish a wide range of high quality large print books including:
Romances, Mysteries, Classics
General Fiction
Non Fiction and Westerns

Special interest titles available in large print are:
The Little Oxford Dictionary
Music Book, Song Book
Hymn Book, Service Book

Also available from us courtesy of Oxford University Press:
Young Readers' Dictionary
(large print edition)
Young Readers' Thesaurus
(large print edition)

For further information or a free brochure, please contact us at:
Ulverscroft Large Print Books Ltd.,
The Green, Bradgate Road, Anstey,
Leicester, LE7 7FU, England.
Tel: (00 44) **0116 236 4325**
Fax: (00 44) **0116 234 0205**

CONVALESCENT HEART

Lynne Collins

They called Romily the Snow Queen, but once she had been all fire and passion, kindled into loving by a man's kiss and sure it would last a lifetime. She still believed it would, for her. It had lasted only a few months for the man who had stormed into her heart. After Greg, how could she trust any man again? So was it likely that surgeon Jake Conway could pierce the icy armour that the lovely ward sister had wrapped about her emotions?

TOO MANY LOVES

Juliet Gray

Justin Caldwell, a famous personality of stage and screen, was blessed with good looks and charm that few women could resist. Stacy was a newcomer to England and she was not impressed by the handsome stranger; she thought him arrogant, ill-mannered and detestable. By the time that Justin desired to begin again on a new footing it was much too late to redeem himself in her eyes, for there had been too many loves in his life.

MYSTERY AT MELBECK

Gillian Kaye

Meg Bowering goes to Melbeck House in the Yorkshire Dales to nurse the rich, elderly Mrs Peacock. She likes her patient and is immediately attracted to Mrs Peacock's nephew and heir, Geoffrey, who farms nearby. But Geoffrey is a gambling man and Meg could never have foreseen the dreadful chain of events which follow. Throughout her ordeal, she is helped by the local vicar, Andrew Sheratt, and she soon discovers where her heart really lies.